CW01190416

BLOOD, SWEAT, AND DESIRE:
A PSYCHOLOGICAL THRILLER

BRITNEY KING

COPYRIGHT

BLOOD, SWEAT, AND DESIRE is a work of fiction. Names, characters, places, images, and incidents are products of the author's imagination or are used fictitiously and are not to be construed as real. Any resemblance to actual events, locales, organizations, persons, living or dead, is entirely coincidental and not intended by the author. The scanning, uploading, and distribution of this book without permission is a theft of the author's intellectual property. No part of this publication may be used, shared or reproduced in any manner whatsoever without written permission except in the case of brief quotations embodied in critical articles and reviews. If you would like permission to use material from the book (other than for review purposes), please contact http://britneyking.com/contact/

Thank you for your support of the author's rights.

Hot Banana Press
Cover Design by Britney King LLC
Cover Image by Snapwire
Copy Editing by Librum Artis
Proofread by Proofreading by the Page

Copyright © 2023 by Britney King LLC. All Rights Reserved.

First Edition: 2023
ISBN 13: 9798852342119
ISBN 10: 8852342119

britneyking.com

"Lovers don't finally meet somewhere.
They're in each other all along."

— Rumi

PROLOGUE

A dream can die so quickly. That's what Michael would later realize, but now he is only thinking how lucky he is, how he's waited his whole life to be here, how this is his time.

Sunlight pierces the delicate veil of dawn, casting a golden hue across the luxurious room. Michael, dressed in his pristine, white chef's uniform, blinks against the harsh light as he studies himself in the mirror. It had been a restless night. He had gotten little in the way of sleep, and it shows in his reflection.

The weight of responsibility bears down upon him; his wealthy clients have paid handsomely for his culinary expertise. This weekend he's been tasked with impressing their friends, and Michael is not one to disappoint.

He glances at the clock—6:30 a.m.—same as always, to meet the Browns' high breakfast expectations.

As Michael enters the kitchen, the scent of yesterday's indulgence still lingers: the rich aroma of garlic, butter, and red wine intermingling with the subtle notes of fresh herbs. He takes a moment to appreciate the quiet solitude before the chaos of the day begins—the soft hum of the refrigerator, the gentle ticking of the clock.

Michael cracks his knuckles and rolls up his sleeves. His movements are precise and efficient, like an orchestra conductor—every tool has its place, and every step is choreographed. This is Michael's domain and sanctuary.

He reaches for the industrial-sized pepper grinder, but whips his arm back at the sight of a crimson stain on the pristine white tiles. His pulse skyrockets and his neck tightens with trepidation as he follows the trail of droplets that lead him to the pantry door.

Please let it be nothing.

Michael knows whatever lies beyond could disrupt his life entirely, yet the compulsion to investigate is too strong to resist.

Gritting his teeth, he grabs the cold metal handle and eases open the door, revealing a scene that sends his heart into his throat.

A man, one of the guests, is slumped against the shelves, a butcher knife lodged in his neck. Blood stains the walls and floor of the pantry like a gruesome masterpiece.

Michael gasps in horror, paralyzed as the metallic scent of blood mingles with the aroma of fresh coffee and pastries, bringing bile up the back of his throat.

"Help!" he cries out, his voice cracking under the weight of shock. "I need help down here!"

Michael's pleas echo through the grand house, and soon doors burst open.

"Michael?" a woman's voice says. He whips around to see his boss standing behind him, her face racked with worry as she clutches a ratty robe tight against her slim frame. Even in chaos, her beauty is undeniable. "What is going on?"

But before he can answer, a guest rushes into the room and gestures toward the grisly path leading to the pantry. "Is that —blood?"

"Everyone, stay back!" Emily's hands tremble as she attempts to remain composed despite the overwhelming situation. Dark circles beneath her eyes show the emotional turmoil she's been put through over the weekend.

Another woman shoves past the others, her lips pursed with determination. But when she reaches the pantry, she stops dead in her tracks.

The guest standing behind her gasps, "My God."

He lunges forward, attempting to cover his wife's eyes from the grisly sight in front of them, but it's too late. She whimpers and stares, aghast at the macabre display. Her gaze scans her friend's faces, trying to comprehend how something like this could have happened.

Michael watches as Jack Brown moves closer, his steely stare evaluating the situation with a businessman's clinical precision. He squats down beside his friend's body and applies two fingers against his neck, feeling for any hint of life beneath the still skin.

The room seems to hold its breath, clinging desperately to hope that this is all a terrible mistake.

"Nothing," he says, shaking his head. "He's dead."

The words drop like a guillotine, slicing through the fragile veneer of denial. Disbelief turns to dread, and Michael can feel the tension in the room ratcheting up another notch, a palpable undercurrent of fear now mingling with their shock.

Emily bursts into sobs. "I don't understand. Who...who would do this?"

She wraps her arms around herself, as though seeking protection from an unseen threat. But just as soon as the sobs start, they subside, and Emily straightens her spine. "Are you sure he's dead, Jack? Check again."

"Trust me," he replies, "you don't fake that kind of injury."

A jolt of panic rushes through the crowd as someone gasps, "Oh my God...there's been an intruder—a home invasion!"

Everyone turns toward the source of the shriek, only to find her frozen in place, wide-eyed and pale.

Michael strides forward. "It's okay," he says confidently, though his voice wavers. "I checked all the doors when I got up. They're still locked."

Emily looks stricken. "What if they're still in the house?"

"That's a possibility," Jack says. "We need to call the police."

Michael swallows hard as he pulls out his cellphone, his fingers hovering over the numbers as if they are burning hot. He wants to make the call—it's the obvious thing to do—but deep down he knows it will change everything.

Will he still have his job? His dream? Everything he has worked so hard for? The Browns' lives will be forever changed, but they will still need to eat, right? So many questions swirl around his mind as he presses the call button.

Michael forgets he's holding his breath until a calm voice on the other end of the line says, "Nine-one-one, what's your emergency?"

He exhales long and slow before speaking. "Hello? Yes, we need help. There's been a murder."

1

Emily

Dead *men cannot tell tales.* My husband's words bounce around my mind as I stand transfixed at the floor-to-ceiling windows of our ostentatious, yet tranquil, living room. I push the thoughts away, turning my attention to the golden hue the setting sun has draped over our manicured lawn. A woman pushing a stroller passes, followed by a little boy on a bike, and my heart swells with a sense of contentment so powerful it borders on overwhelming.

God, I love this house.

I imagine what it will be like, knowing that soon that woman will be me.

Jack's footsteps echo from the hallway, reminding me of the life we've built together—outwardly successful and surprisingly easy, at that.

"Em, they're here," he announces, as if I didn't hear the tires crunching on the gravel driveway. "I opened the gate."

Rachel's electric blue convertible arrives first, followed by Lucas's practical sedan, Sarah and Will's sleek black SUV, and finally Ava's modest hatchback. I watch as my friends converge on the driveway, each bringing their own distinct energy.

"Time to play hostess," I say to Jack, wearing a sly smile on my lips as I open the front door. We've just made love in the guest bathroom, and the flush still lingers on my husband's cheeks. Instinctively, my hand brushes my stomach, and I wonder if this will be the time it happens.

"Emily!" Rachel squeals as I throw open the door. Her eyes scan me up and down before she pulls me in for a tight embrace. "You look fabulous, as always," she gushes before taking a deep whiff of the air around us. "And whatever that smell is," she closes her eyes and looks heavenward, "my God! It's divine!"

"Thanks, Rach," I reply, easing out of her embrace. "But I can't take credit. It's all Michael's doing."

"Michael?" She cocks her head. "Who's Michael?"

"Our new chef." Jack grins proudly. "My wife can't stop raving about him. I keep telling Em she'd better keep it down or someone's going to steal him out from under us."

My best friend's lips curl into a smile. "That someone might be me."

I scan the group of faces. Lucas is beaming warmly, Sarah's clinging to Will like a lifeline, and Ava is standing alone, her expression unreadable.

"Come on in," I say, gesturing them inside. Voices and laughter surge through the living room as they settle in, while I observe the interactions between them; an invisible weight presses against their words.

Lucas nods in approval. "Emily, you've outdone yourself—but then you always do, don't you?"

"Thanks, Lucas," I reply with a shrug. "It's not me; I just hire well."

I catch a hint of skepticism in his eyes, but he says nothing more.

Will jumps into the conversation with enthusiasm, producing a bottle of wine from behind his back. "Jack mentioned you got a new car? How's it treating you?" His blue eyes sparkle with anticipation as he sets the bottle on the coffee table.

A glow spreads across my face as I remember the test drive; the rapture of speed coursing through my veins like an electric current. "Like a dream," I say breathlessly.

Will's lips spread into a wide grin, his eyes alight with understanding. I see the same excitement I feel in my chest reflected. "Ah, the thrill of speed. I know that feeling."

"Will finds a new method of speed every month," Sarah says flatly. She fidgets in her seat, her eyes darting around the room like a frightened animal looking for an escape route.

"Don't be too jealous, Sarah," Ava says. "The car is just Jack's way of distracting Em from her bout of baby fever."

"I'm not sure anything could distract my wife," Jack says with a shake of his head. "Not even a beautiful car. You know how it is—when Emily gets something in her head, watch out; nothing better get in her way."

He leans down and plants a kiss on my forehead. "Right, honey?"

Not really, I want to say. If that were the case, I'd be pregnant instead of feeling like a failure month after month when it doesn't happen. But this is not the time or the place for this conversation. Everything still feels too raw. Panic surfaces, and instead of responding, I blurt out quickly, "Would you guys like something to drink?"

Ava shatters the silence first as expected. "Something strong for me, please." She puts up a steely facade, but I've known her forever. I can see the heartache that glazes her features. It fills the air like foggy moisture. She misses Brian. We all do. Our gatherings feel emptier—quieter—without him.

"Well, I wish you guys would get on it," Sarah quips. "Will and I are tired of being the only ones with kids."

"We're working on it," I say, handing Ava a full glass tumbler. "That's the fun part, right?" When our fingers brush briefly, I see relief wash over Ava's face before she looks away.

"She wouldn't know," Ava says. "It happened for them on the first try."

This time it's me who looks away, who searches for a way out. "Excuse me. I'd better check on dinner."

The smell of garlic and rosemary wafts through the air as I step into the kitchen to check in with Michael, simultaneously watching Jack and Will from the corner of my eye. When I walk back out into the living area, it's clear their conversation has taken on an unmistakable edge as they discuss their latest professional accomplishments. I can't help but roll my eyes at their thinly veiled competitiveness; it's almost as if they're comparing the size of their...paychecks.

"Of course, the real key to getting the deal was anticipating their counter-arguments ahead of time," Jack says, his tone dripping with smug satisfaction.

"Ah, yes," Will responds, studying the glass of wine in his hand. "That's always been a strength of yours, hasn't it? Thinking three steps ahead."

"Speaking of thinking ahead," Lucas interjects, his voice soft yet firm, "what's the plan for this weekend?"

I'm not surprised Lucas brings it up first. He likes gaining his wife's approval just as much as the rest of us. Rachel has spent innumerable hours planning this getaway, and these weekends are important to her—always have been, since college. We've skipped a few years due to various life events, including Will and Sarah having a baby, but Rach is adamant that this getaway will put us back on track.

I've tried breaking it to her that we're not in college anymore. We're not twenty-somethings with all that time on our hands and all that life yet to be lived. We're in a different stage now, with busy careers and *real* adult responsibilities. It's not as easy to break away as it once was. And I do often worry it may never be again. My best friend, as well intentioned as she may be, seems to be the only one who can't—who *refuses*—to see that.

"It's just *one* weekend," Rachel quips. "You all act like I'm asking for a kidney or something."

"No, seriously," Lucas says, coming to her aid. "What's everyone thinking?"

A silent tension fills the room as we anxiously await an answer that never comes.

2

Jack

Everyone's buzzing about the plan for this weekend, and all I can think about is how to get out of it.

But that's not the only thing I'm thinking. There's a lot on my mind. Like how I'm going to slowly dismember the idiot who's sitting on my couch, seducing everyone with his charm. Next, he's going to devour my food as though he doesn't already owe me enough as it is. The *audacity*.

I knew better than to have trusted him, but I went against my instincts, just like I'm doing now by having that snake in our home. When I mentioned this to Emily, she brushed me off and said, "A snake doesn't know it's a snake, Jack. It just is."

"So?"

"So, sometimes you have to let it be."

I was annoyed, but it reminded me why I love Em. It's nice to have a voice of reason. Where I like to move fast, my wife moves slow. She takes everything into account, whereas I say done is better than perfect.

"What's the plan for this weekend?" Lucas probes once more.

Everyone's eyes dart around, expecting someone else to answer. I don't know about them, but personally, I've got big plans. I've been waiting all evening to tell Em, but she had other ideas, and now we have these people sitting around our living room. She calls them friends; I call them a waste of time.

One of them, Ava, scrambles for an answer to Lucas's question, her eyebrows knitting together in confusion, as if she has forgotten. But before her lips part to speak, her eyes glimmer mischievously. Stillness fills the room as we await her response. Finally, she throws her hands up and laughs boisterously. "It's a joke, Rach! We all know what this weekend is. You've dominated the group chat for months."

Rachel gives a sardonic smile and downs the rest of her wine.

Have I mentioned I really hate these people?

There are so many other things I could be doing right now. Starting with the incident I tried to talk to Emily about earlier, when she ignored and then seduced me.

Lucas persists, raising an eyebrow at my wife. "It's not a difficult question…what I'm asking is when is everyone planning on driving out?"

"Early afternoon, right, Jack?" Emily responds, glancing my way. "I just need to pick up a few last-minute things tomorrow."

She has no idea.

Rachel stands tall, her red lips poising her for battle. "Lucas and I have already packed," she declares, throwing down the gauntlet. Or so she thinks. Rachel's bravado is more showy than scary. She's the type who always needs to talk to the manager, who wants everyone to know who she is, and thinks they already do. Or at least they should. "We'll be ready to leave bright and early Friday morning."

Her gaze dares anyone to challenge her plan.

I'm not interested in challenging her, but she sure would be fun to murder. I told Em this once, but only once, and let's just say it's a topic that's off limits. "Our friends are untouchable," she'd said. "No matter what."

I remember laughing. But I'm not laughing now.

"Actually," Sarah mumbles, clinging to Will's arm, "I'm not sure I'll be able to make it this weekend."

That makes two of us.

"Of course you can," Rachel counters. Her gaze is as sharp as a razor and her tone implies Sarah's preference for solitude is absurd. "You deserve a break more than any of us. Besides, the estate I rented is *enormous*. You'll find plenty of quiet corners to hide away in, if that's what you want."

Actually, that could work.

"Fine," Sarah concedes, her shoulders drooping under the weight of Rachel's insistence. "I'll see what I can do."

I can relate. Earlier, just when I thought I had everything figured out, Emily looked at me with those doe eyes of hers, batted her lashes, and pleaded with me; and before I knew it, my belt was unfastened. I wanted to talk, my wife wanted to fuck. It's not every day a man gets this lucky. Believe me, I know. Not a day goes by that I am not reminded of my good fortune.

So, yeah, I'll be the first to admit, I may be a sucker when it comes to Em, but I refuse to be a pushover in any other area of my life. Even Emily knows I have my limits where she's concerned.

My thoughts drift back to the day we met— it was the happiest moment of my life, and in many ways, I've been chasing it ever since. Possibly, so has she.

Like many marriages, it's easy when it's easy, and it's hell when it's not. I realize this isn't saying much, but that's love. It can't be summed up with a neat little bow. And in any case, no one loves like Emily does. Just ask any of these assholes taking up space in my house. She's like a fucking magnet, the way she effortlessly draws people in. I love that about her, but I hate it too. Sometimes it feels like Emily's the sun, and we're all just circling her orbit. It's exhausting and exhilarating at the same time. But it sure as hell makes it difficult to be discreet.

I know sometimes Em just wants to live a "normal" life, so I go along with her ideas, no matter how ridiculous they may be—dinner parties, these insipid fake friends she insists she likes but really just make her feel better about herself...even this house in this neighborhood full of sheep. All of it, I do for her.

But we are not, nor will we ever be, normal people. And sooner or later, she's going to realize that.

3

Emily

I wouldn't dare back out of Rachel's weekend getaway, but that doesn't stop the others from trying. True to form, Rachel beats them into submission until any and all objections are silenced. I love that about her. I once read that we pick the people closest to us based upon the traits we are lacking, and it makes sense. Anytime I am near Rach, I am reminded of the disparities between us. As a matter of fact, I'm pretty sure she has this effect on everyone.

I listen as Sarah backtracks. Sarah promises Rachel she'll figure it out, that she wouldn't miss Rachel's weekend for anything.

"Excellent," Rach says, her smile triumphant. "Now, let's finalize the menu for Saturday night's dinner. I want everything to be absolutely perfect."

As she launches into a detailed plan involving caviar and soufflés, I can't help but marvel at her ability to take control of any situation. It's both impressive and exhausting. In the midst of her culinary soliloquy, my phone vibrates in my pocket. I glance at Jack and decide to ignore it. He hates when I take work calls after hours, and considering we're trying to start a family, I realize he has a point. It's best to put guardrails in place now.

The moment Rachel finishes her monologue, Will's laughter cuts through the air like a whip, his commanding presence snatching everyone's attention. His arm moves from Sarah's grip, and he strides toward the bar cart with smooth confidence.

"Emily," he offers, his voice deep and inviting. "Would you care for a refill?"

I know Jack doesn't want him here, and I think Will knows it too. My cheeks start to burn as I walk over, handing him my empty wineglass. "Uh, sure. Thanks."

"Of course." His blue eyes sparkle mischievously as he takes it from me, and I feel the walls start to close in. I can feel Jack's thoughts from here.

"I'm really excited about this getaway Rachel has planned," Will says. "We could all use a break, don't you think?"

Across the room, laughter brings a moment of relief, but it's short-lived. "Yeah, it's been awhile," I remark. "It's been what, three years since our last friends' trip?"

"Four," Ava says quietly, her gaze fixed on the floor as she holds out her glass for another round. Anxiety ripples through me; we've all noticed her fragile mental state lately, and I worry that more wine won't help the situation. One second, she's quiet and sad, the next she's arrogant and rude. Add alcohol and it's a disaster in the making.

Last time we hosted dinner, Ava ended up in our guest room and ruined half the linens. She cut her wrist, and though the wound was superficial, it was a wake-up call for us all. Well, everyone except Jack. He was none too pleased that Ava would pull such a "stunt" here. The epitome of self-control, he simply cannot understand someone letting themselves go to the extent Ava has. Did this cause a bit of a rift between us? Maybe. But I can't deny he has a point. Ava refuses to seek help, so Jack is right about one thing—there's not a whole lot I can do.

"Four," I echo, my eyes brimming with concern. Will hands me a freshly refilled glass of red, his fingers brushing against mine. I tell myself it was an accident, but I can see that he and Jack haven't settled their differences, and I know Will feels inferior. I tried to tell my husband it was not a good idea to do business with friends, but he just gave me that signature smug look of his and said, "Why not? What better way to find out who they *really* are?"

Across the room, Rachel raises her glass in a toast, catching my attention, catching *everyone's* attention. "Here's to a weekend we won't forget!"

"Cheers," I say before taking a sip, my eyes still on Will. What is it about him that has me so unbalanced? My loyalty to Jack has never wavered, and it unsettles me completely. One thing is for sure, I will not allow them to make me a pawn in their game.

My phone buzzes in my pocket and I take it out, expecting another mundane message from my assistant or an alert about a calendar reminder. Instead, I find a cryptic warning: "Good luck this weekend. You're gonna need it."

My chest tightens as I read the words again, trying to comprehend them. I scan the room, my gaze shifting between each of my friends, wondering who sent this and why. I search their faces, seeking any trace of guilt or trickery. But their countenances remain placid, their eyes fixed on one another, and I realize it might have been Jack.

The games he plays.

"Everything okay, Em?" Jack asks, his voice tinged with concern.

"Uh, yeah." I force a smile. "Just a work thing."

"Ah, always working." He shakes his head in mild reproach. This is my husband's idea of foreplay. "Can't you leave it behind for one night?"

I look over as I trail my nails up his back, digging just a little. If that's what he wants, fine, I'll bite. "Not a chance."

4

Anonymous

A fierce gust of wind screams through the window, bringing with it an ache of despair that reverberates in my soul. I'm transfixed by her; she's like a hurricane in the middle of the room. Her long chestnut hair frames her delicate face, and her ripe lips curl as she speaks to her husband. I cannot look away.

My lungs seize as I stare at him: a dull figure, his features contorted by anger and pomposity into something unrecognizable. His wrathful eyes are full of self-importance and entitlement —stealing away from her all that love she deserves. Jealousy floods me, a scorching lava snaking through my veins at the thought of possessing her, breaking her down, providing her with a different kind of love than what he denies her.

He may have money, but his wealth cannot protect her from someone as ambitious as I am.

It really is too bad.

He will never experience even a fraction of the beauty and

spirit that brands itself onto my heart each time I lock eyes with her. The atmosphere between us is electric with anticipation. It's like I'm standing in the crater of a live volcano, waiting for the inevitable eruption.

Soon she will be mine—a captive of my making. I won't rest until she is under my control and I can show her the pleasure that awaits if she just gives in. But that's not the only truth she needs to discover...

5

Jack

The engine purrs like a kitten as I slide along the empty highway, trying to silence my reservations about the trip. Em is entranced by her victory and oozes seduction with every movement. Her nipples harden through the thin fabric of her dress as she turns toward me, a mischievous smirk playing on her lips. I can feel the heat radiating off her body, and my willpower dissolves. I try to remind myself of the reasons I shouldn't give in, but her hand on my thigh distracts me. I can't resist her touch, and I find myself leaning into her, drawn by her magnetic energy.

"Are you nervous?" she asks, her voice low and sultry.

I cannot lie to my wife, even if I want to. "No."

Her lips brush against my ear. "You should be."

I can't help but smile. Emily and her many faces. I suppose I shouldn't be surprised by it, not after this long together, but to her credit, I often am. I assume this is how she's done, and continues to do, so well in life. One moment, she's meek and quiet, my perfect little mouse, the next she's a fucking lioness, fierce and independent, forever outsmarting her prey.

My desire rises as my eyes meet hers. Her beauty is unmatched, and the way she carries herself screams confidence. But this feeling is different from any before it; something electric between us that compels me to act on it.

I reach over and brush my hand against her thigh, feeling the warmth through the thin fabric of her dress. Em lets out a soft gasp, but she doesn't back away from me. My fingers slowly inch up her leg toward her dress until they meet resistance; skin on skin. She moans softly as my digits trace circles around her clitoris, and I can tell she is desperate for me to pull off the road.

I take the next exit and screech into a gas station, parking around back. I don't hesitate before grabbing Em and crushing my lips against hers. Our mouths clash together in a passionate frenzy as I tug at her dress, lifting it up over her hips.

One second I'm fastened in the driver's seat, the next I'm halfway in hers. I plunge my face between her creamy thighs, tasting her. She bucks against my face as she comes undone, her moans echoing through the parking lot.

We take it to the backseat. Our mouths explore one another's bodies with hungry urgency as I thrust deep within her and our skin slams together with each stroke.

When we're done, a heavy silence blankets the car until Em breaks it. "I know there's something you want to tell me. I can feel it."

That's the other thing about my wife—she has this supernatural power that goes beyond a woman's intuition. She's psychic, and for better or worse, she knows me all too well. "I have someone in mind," I confess. "You're going to like this one."

"I'm sure," she says, fastening her bra. Em knows when I'm trying to sell her on an idea, and it's a turn off. Sometimes I can't help myself. "But can we just get through this weekend?"

"Sure."

"Then we can talk about it."
"Of course."
"Dr. Bell called."
"Yeah?"
"My tests came back. Everything looked normal." She lets out a long sigh. "He said sometimes it just takes time."
I smile. "I hadn't expected any different."
She glances toward the station, eyes narrowing. "I'm going to run in and use the ladies' room. Need anything?"
"No. I'll fill up while you're in there."
I know Em will think this was all planned, that what happens next, I did on purpose. But it's not true—people like this exist all over. It takes a certain kind of naivety to bring a child into this world, but Emily wants a baby, and no amount of understanding can change that fact.

She no longer sees the world the way I do, and despite the fact that I can't imagine living my life without her, I'm beginning to wonder if that's a problem we can overcome.

I step around the car and pause before locking eyes with the gas attendant. He looks off, like a creep. Still, I know better than to judge by appearances alone, and all hypothesis must be tested. I slip my phone onto the hood of the car and duck into the passenger seat, out of sight; thieves are everywhere these days. It takes only seconds before I realize my instincts were right.

One reach into the console and I'm gripping the injector pen full of ricin tightly in my fist as I face the stranger again. "Excuse me," I say, "did you see a phone laying here?"

The man shakes his head and sucks in air through his teeth.

I take another step forward, positioning the pen so that if he puts up a fight, I am not at risk.

Just then, a hand rests gently on my shoulder, and I freeze. "There you are, honey," Emily says. I turn to find her standing behind me, holding out a water bottle.

"Wait in the car," I say firmly.

"Jack..." She shifts from one foot to the other.

"Please."

"We'll be late." Her eyes plead with me. "Just let it go."

"He has my phone."

"It's a decoy, love. Let. It. Go."

"I can't. You know I can't."

She huffs and rolls her eyes. "Fine."

I watch as Em flips on her heel and walks in the creep's direction. "Excuse me, would you mind taking our picture?"

She hands the guy her phone, leaning a little too close for my comfort. I've always known my wife to be a little crazy, but she has to know we're already on camera. We don't need an extra memento.

The creep takes the picture, and Emily examines it to make sure it meets her standards. With a smile and a nod, she thanks the stranger.

As soon as we get into the car, she chucks both her phone and the decoy into my lap. "You want to know what I'm thinking?"

I don't have to answer. Of course I want to know what she is thinking. I always want to know what she is thinking. But somehow, there's something inside her I can't quite reach.

"I took his photo," she continues. "And I got your decoy back."

"Two birds, one stone," I say, but Em knows this is not what I wanted. This was not the goal. It will change nothing.

"When we get home," she says, "you're going to use Google Reverse Image Search over both Tor and a VPN to locate him through social media."

"Okay."

"Then you're going to wait one year from today."

I nod in agreement, although I'm not sure why we have to wait a whole year.

She fastens her seatbelt. "We have a lot going on."

"Do we?"

Em smiles, and I swear it lights up the entire sky. "One year from today, you're going to leave your real phone at home, and you're going to go to his house."

"Then what?"

"Guess."

The pieces click together, and I smile back, remembering our past. I realize what my wife is doing. I also realize how wrong I've been. She hasn't changed. This is a throwback to how we met.

The funny thing is, I know it isn't just about that creep. It is about Em and me. It is about our connection, our desire to protect one another. In the end, it's about more than just a phone. It's about love. It's about going the distance.

6

Emily

The car screeches to a halt in front of the lavish mansion, its grandeur dazzling like a mirage. I fling open the door and leap out, my eyes widening with excitement. The air smells of grass and sea salt as we take in the breathtaking sight of the ocean and the roar of the waves crashing violently below.

They remind me of my husband's mood. I suppose I should have let him have his way back at the gas station, but I didn't want any potential complications. Besides, I knew it would be all he would want to talk about, and frankly, I just don't have it in me. At the same time, if an itch needs to be scratched, maybe I should have let him scratch it. I don't know.

Sometimes, the way Jack looks at me, it's like he thinks I have it all figured out, like there's some grand plan, when really, like most things in life, I'm just making it up as I go.

I figured by this point in a marriage one should have all the answers, but more often than not, I feel just as clueless as the day we met.

Suffice to say, I have never been more desperate for a break, just to get away from it all. What a relief it is to be here. This place is perfect.

"Welcome to paradise!" Rachel whoops, skipping out to the driveway. She throws her arms wide open. "Let's make this weekend one for the books!"

"Rachel, this place is extraordinary," I say. "You did an incredible job—"

"Only the best for my favorite people," she says with a wink, and soon it's not just Jack and Rachel and me in the drive. Everyone has arrived.

Once pleasantries and room assignments are dished out, everyone races off to explore the mansion, and I stroll into the kitchen. I find Michael by the marble countertop. His dark hair is pulled back in a neat ponytail, and his deep-set eyes are laser-focused on his vegetables, slicing with surgical precision. It isn't long before the rest of the group wanders in.

Jack strides in last. "I took our bags to the room," he says, kissing my cheek. "Is dinner ready? I'm starving."

"Everyone," I announce proudly. "You remember Michael? Well, surprise! He's our chef for the weekend."

My friends gather around him, their faces alight with curiosity and awe as they see the variety of ingredients scattered around him. Questions about his menu roll off their tongue while I step back, pleased with myself for making such a brilliant choice.

Michael lifts his head from his work and gazes at me with a heart-warming smile. "Thank you, Emily," he says above everyone's chatter. "I will do everything possible to make this an unforgettable weekend."

"Smells like success to me." Will's booming voice drags me in like an undertow, a feeling that pulses through my veins with an electric energy. I can feel Jack tense beside me as his eyes take on a strange intensity, but Rachel claps her hands to regain our attention.

"Let's give Michael some space to work his magic," she says, herding us out of the room. "The garden outside is the perfect spot for pre-dinner drinks! Wait till you see it!"

As we move toward the door, I catch Jack's gaze lingering on Will for a moment as we exit the room. Uneasy with the strange tension between our friend and my husband, I try to suppress the growing suspicion that this weekend will be anything but wonderful.

Through gritted teeth, I offer a toast: "Here's to a time filled with laughter, love, and unforgettable memories."

But Jack isn't biting. Instead he just remarks matter-of-factly, "We could have stayed home for that."

"Don't be such a party pooper." Ava bumps him playfully. "The rest of us would like to spend some time with Em, too."

She links her arm with mine, and we step out the back door, where the last of the remaining daylight gives an otherworldly luminescence to the outdoor patio. We take our assigned seats, and soon the roar of laughter and clinking glasses fills the air. It's a great start to a lovely evening. Unfortunately, I get the feeling dinner isn't the only thing about to be served.

7

Emily

Michael proudly places the platter in the center of the table, the succulent scallops perfectly seared and the saffron risotto a work of art. "Bon appétit," he announces with a smile that could charm even the most discerning food critic. The scent of white wine and garlic tantalizes my nose as I take a bite, savoring every rich, buttery flavor.

"Emily, I'm so glad you brought Michael," Rachel beams. "I can't help but think I should hire him—when he's not with you guys, of course."

"You know I love you," I reply, my gaze shifting to the chef who has retreated to the house. "But you're not stealing my new favorite person."

"I've been dethroned," Jack interjects. "Guess I'd better learn to cook."

"You have many other talents," I say, intertwining my fingers with his. "I'd prefer you focused on those…"

"You guys have been married too long to act like newlyweds," Rachel teases as the banter continues between us. Lucas regales us with stories from college while Ava shares her wild days as a flight attendant, until Rachel interrupts, waving her wineglass in the air for attention.

"All right, all right," she announces with a wicked grin on her lips. "I have an idea, something that'll make this weekend unforgettable."

She pauses, a devilish grin playing at the corners of her lips. "You know how these weekends go—it's always us girls off to one side of the house, you men on the other. Well, I was thinking... What if we did something a little different?"

I am thinking different as in a scavenger hunt or a hike at dawn. Certainly nothing at all like what comes out of her mouth next.

"What if..." Rachel says, "we did a spouse swap?"

The table falls silent, the atmosphere suddenly charged with intrigue and uncertainty. I can feel my heart race at the mere mention of such a taboo suggestion. The faces around me reflect an array of reactions, from shock to curiosity, amusement to skepticism. I can't wait to skip to the part where my best friend announces she's joking.

"Rachel..." Lucas says, his voice tinged with caution. "What are you even saying?"

"I think we need to cut her off," Jack suggests. "Sounds like she's found her limit."

"Come on, guys," Rachel insists, her cheeks flushed from both the wine and the audacity of her proposal. "We're all friends here! We can explore something new, something thrilling! It doesn't have to be sexual—just the joy of being with someone different! Something to make us appreciate what we have."

Ava shudders, obviously not excited about Rachel's suggestion.

But I realize then that Rachel isn't joking. Nor will she give up easily. "Let's draw names from a hat! We can make it a game...the couple to stay up the longest wins—"

    She looks at Lucas. "What do you say honey, ten grand?"

    He shrugs. "Sure. Why not?"

    "Ten grand just for staying awake?" Jack chides.

    Rachel rolls her eyes. "Well, no. I mean, you actually have to be interesting enough to the person you're paired with to keep them awake for forty-eight hours straight."

    I can't help but smile. "I came here to rest."

    "Think about it!" Rachel says, "You only live once. Variety is the spice of life!"

I glance around the table, observing my friends as they consider the possibilities. Some seem intrigued by Rachel's words, while others wage an internal battle between curiosity and caution. As for me? I'm completely torn—unable to deny the allure of competition, but also wary of its consequences.

"Look, I'm not saying we need to *do* anything—it can be totally PG—and we don't have to decide right now," Rachel continues, noticing the group's apprehension. "Let's finish up dinner, enjoy ourselves tonight and if anyone is game for my idea later, well... we'll tackle that when we come to it."

Rachel's words drop like a bomb, exploding in the air and rippling through us with an almost electric charge. I can feel the tension simmering beneath the surface of our laughter and conversation, the unspoken question lingering on everyone's lips: Will we or won't we?

But for now, we continue eating, drinking, and sharing stories, though each of us knows that the night has taken an unexpected turn.

8

Emily

The candlelight flickers against our faces as we dig into the fourth course. We all seem to have had a few drinks too many, and the laughter grows louder with each passing hour. I can't help but think of Rachel's offer. The thought lingers in my mind like a snake coiled around my skull, whispering wicked suggestions. I don't need the money, but it would be nice to have. If nothing else, just to say I won.

It doesn't help that Will is across the table entrancing me with his sly grins and sparkling eyes. His voice is hypnotic, sending chills through my body that awaken something long dormant inside me. I know better, but that doesn't stop the curiosity from bubbling to the surface. I may be married, and I'm obviously hopelessly in love with my husband, but I'm still human.

Sometimes it's nice to remember there was a me before all of this. That something as simple and complex as attraction with a person you hardly know can still exist.

"Did you hear about the time Lucas tried to catch a fish with his bare hands?" Will says, drawing us all in. I join in on the laughter, though I'm not sure why it's so funny.

I glance at Jack, who has become unusually quiet. "Jack, honey, are you okay?"

He adjusts uncomfortably in his seat, only flashing an artificial smile. It's perplexing how stoic he's been since arriving here, like a secret diary with unturned pages.

"Of course," he mumbles, above the clinking of silverware. "Just thinking."

"Remember when Emily told Jack she was training for a marathon with us but ended up going to the movies every weekend instead?" Ava pipes up.

"What? It was a really great era of film," I confess with a laugh at her recollection. I glance at my husband and add, "Nothing like the crap they're pushing on us today."

Jack seems indifferent to the comment I made on his behalf, which tells me everything I need to know. But even while analyzing my husband's impossible moods, I can't help but pick up on Sarah's nervous stance. Her fingers turn pale from clutching onto her fork too tightly. Her stare remains affixed to her plate. She refuses to look up at anyone.

"Lucas, don't you think this swap thing is a bit extreme, even for Rach?" Ava pushes her voice up a notch. She's had one too many, and she's looking to pick a fight with Rachel by going through her husband. "I mean, what happened to normal stuff like board games or movies? Even bad ones…"

Lucas defends Rachel's idea, his brow furrowing. "Who's to say it won't be fun?"

"I do," Ava says sharply. "I say."

Lucas shrugs her off. "It could be interesting. Trying something new can be exhilarating. Plus, there's ten grand up for grabs. You know, easy money."

"No one at this table even gets out of bed for ten grand," Ava counters. "It's chump change."

"I guess we shall see," he counters.

The spat between Lucas and Ava accelerates, their words slicing the air like knives, making me increasingly uncomfortable. Sarah casts Will an uneasy and sad look from the corner of her eye.

"Hey, guys, let's not argue about this," I interject, attempting to defuse the situation. "Rachel's just drunk. I wouldn't read too much into it."

"Fine," Ava sniffs, folding her arms firmly across her chest. "Let's just pretend like everyone hasn't completely lost their minds and enjoy the rest of our dinner."

Ava uses sarcasm like a weapon, but it's almost like she wills peace into existence. At least temporarily. The conversation starts up again, though all I can focus on is Jack.

What's he thinking?
Surely, he wouldn't do anything stupid.
What kind of game are we playing?
Was it a mistake bringing him here?

When I look at him, he's staring off into the distance, his expression unreadable. It feels like I'm looking at a stranger, not knowing what lies beneath the surface. Am I trying to make him jealous by laughing a little too eagerly at Will's jokes? Maybe. Either way, with each passing moment, the shadows deepen and the tension between us heightens, making me feel suffocated and anxious.

I fill my glass until its brim is overflowing with wine, not enough to get me drunk, but just enough to numb the sharp edges of my emotions. "Enjoying yourself?" Jack asks, leaning over and kissing my temple.

"Sure." I offer a shrug as my eyes scan our company of friends. My husband rarely ever joins us these days, yet here he is—an unwilling participant in our weekend away. I can feel his discomfort, like a tangible force pressing against me from all sides. "Are you?"

"I'm here because you want me to be—I'd do anything for you, Em. You know that."

I realize that Jack has never cared to be as engaged with our group of friends as I have, but he's rarely *this* withdrawn. I can see he's placating me—that he'd rather be *anywhere* else but here.

"I know that," I say. My fingers trace the etchings on the glass, the cool crystal relieving my anxiety. I take a sip of the velvety red, and it flows like liquid courage down my throat. I can feel a shift in the air—it's as if something is coming that could change everything. "Let's go home."

He stares back at me in surprise. "What? And miss all the fun?"

But I'm no longer listening. My mind is miles ahead, already racing to safety.

9

Jack

The wind licks the ivy-strewn patio, making the plants sway like a chorus line. Rachel grins wickedly, reminding me why I've never liked her. "All right, who's in?"

Lucas speaks up, his arm possessively draped around the empty chair beside him. He and Rachel meet each other's gaze with a knowing intensity. "Count us in," he says, in a way that makes it obvious this isn't the first time he's heard about his wife's idea. I wonder, did Lucas plant this in Rachel's head, or was it the other way around?

Will pipes up too, his hungry gaze devouring my wife as if she were prey. A fiery rage wells within me at his nerve; I can barely contain myself. Finally, he glances at Sarah. "Us too."

My eyes drift to Sarah, whose lips are pressed into a tight line, though no words leave her mouth. I know they need the money, as insignificant as it might be to the rest of us. But I also know for that weasel of a husband of hers, this is about more than just the money.

I clear my throat, and all attention shifts to me. Emily looks panicked; I savor every ounce of discomfort radiating from her body. "Emily, what do you think? Are we... participating?"

The air feels heavy like a damp blanket, each breath more labored than the last. We remain suspended in time until finally Emily breaks the silence; gently shaking her head, she says, "I don't think so. I'm tired...I would be a pretty boring partner."

Rachel's face contorts in disbelief and disappointment. "Oh, come on!"

Lucas feigns disappointment. "Darn. I was hoping some other bloke would get to experience Rach's forty-step nighttime skincare routine and her horrendous but very charming snore."

Rachel slaps his arm. "I play to win, my love. No one will be hearing anything." Then she turns to Emily. "Don't let us down now, Em...remember when you used to be fun?"

My wife thinks her friend's words are meant to be harmless, but I know better. I can see the sting and not just because of the flicker of recognition Em sees in my eyes.

Emily hesitates. "Jack," she whispers, voice shaking, "What do you think?"

"It's up to you."

"Like I said, I'd be terrible company... I'll be out the second my head hits the pillow."

Ava snorts. "Yet you didn't say no."

Emily shifts uneasily, and for the first time I have an inkling of what she is thinking—that this is foolish, that nothing will come of it. She's thinking we've all been friends since college; we're more like family at this point. She's thinking this is a joke—as in, it's not actually going to happen. Em isn't taking Rachel's proposal seriously. She doesn't think anyone is.

But she's wrong.

And me? For me, it's personal.

"All right," I say, "We're in."

Emily's head snaps in my direction, shock etched in her features. She starts to speak, but Rachel beats her to the punch. "Excellent!" Rachel claps her hands together. "So, how do we decide who goes with whom?"

"Let's let fate decide," Will suggests, scanning the table for an instrument of destiny. He spots a silver candelabrum, its flickering flames casting dancing shadows across his face. "We'll draw matches. Shortest match chooses their partner first."

"Sounds fair," Lucas agrees, excitement and trepidation mingling in his voice.

Will plucks a match from the candelabrum.

"No," Rachel says. "We draw names—that's how fate decides."

Will nods, yanking a pen and some fancy gilded napkins out of the table setting. "Gentlemen, write your names on these and fold them up. The ladies will draw."

We scribble our names, our destinies tucked away in the folds. Will collects them and places them in an empty crystal wine glass with a flourish.

"Shall we begin?" Rachel asks, her voice buzzing with excitement.

"Definitely." Will extends the wineglass to my wife, and I want to gut him in the most painful way possible. "Ladies first."

Emily hesitates, her fingers hovering over the bunched-up napkins. She gives me a knowing glance, and I can see that Rachel's idea starts to feel different. It starts to feel real, like we're actually doing this, like maybe we're playing with fire.

Even so, I'm not entirely sure she dislikes the feeling. She has that look in her eyes, the same look she had back at the gas station, the same look she gets when she drives the new car I bought her down an open road.

"Pick one," Rachel urges, and Em grabs a napkin, unfolding it to reveal her fate. I know what it says before she reads it. The name stares back at her, an omen written in ink.

"Will," she breathes. A strange cocktail of emotions plays across her face. Excitement? Guilt? Fear? I can't be sure.

"Ah, well." Will's smirk grows wider, his eyes never leaving Emily's. "It's fate, I guess."

My wife doesn't understand what this is about, this ridiculous challenge, but I do. I will never let him win.

The rest of the group takes their turns, each drawing a name and revealing their partner for the night. The tension in the room reaches a palpable crescendo as the last name is drawn.

"All right, everyone," Rachel announces, raising her glass. "To fate, and to new experiences."

The clinking of glasses punctures the air like a pact made in blood. I glance at Emily and she smiles, but it doesn't reach her eyes, and I wonder if she knows what she's gotten herself into.

10

Anonymous

The salty sea air teases my nostrils as I stand alone in the parlor, gazing out the open patio doors at the churning ocean below. An unnatural stillness has settled over the rented sprawling estate, a temporary reprieve before chaos inevitably descends upon this place.

My fingers curl into fists at my sides, nails biting into flesh, as a familiar restlessness rises within. The urge to act, to do something—*anything*—to shatter the fragile peace threatens to overtake me. I tamp it down through sheer force of will, knowing now is not yet the time. Patience. I must have patience.

The ornate furnishings of the parlor mock me with their opulence, gaudy symbols of wealth and status that mean nothing in the end. We're all just meat and bone, flesh and sinew. Mortal. Fallible. Corruptible.

Voices drift in from the foyer, muted laughter and idle chatter.

My lip curls at the sound. Fools, all of them. So unaware of the snakes in their midst, of the darkness that lurks within each soul. If only they could see as I see. Know as I know.

Compulsion rises once more, writhing beneath my skin, demanding release. I squeeze my eyes shut against the urge, digging fingernails into my palms. *Not yet. Your time is coming.*

The chatter grows louder as the group makes their way into the parlor for the evening's entertainment. I paste a smile onto my face and turn to greet them, a perfect mask of congeniality hiding the rage and madness simmering below.

Let the games begin.

Then she glides into view, a vision in crimson silk that clings to every curve. Rage and desire war within me as I watch her work the room, charming everyone with a coy smile or sultry glance.

Mine.

The beast within snarls its claim, fighting against the bonds of civility and reason holding it back. Not yet, not yet, the frantic mantra pounds through my skull in time with my racing pulse.

"Darling, you're staring again."

A hand closes over my arm, the contact jolting me from my fixation. I turn to my side, brows raised in knowing amusement. My lips peel back from my teeth in a parody of a smile as I struggle to rein in the madness churning inside.

"Just admiring the view," I say, tilting my head toward the open patio doors. The excuse is weak, but it is accepted with an easy chuckle, and my arm is released to grab a drink from the chef's passing tray.

Idiot.

If he only knew what was right in front of him, the viper's nest he's blindly wandered into. But he won't see, not until it's too late. They never do.

Finally, she glances up, meeting my eyes from under thick

lashes, a secret smile curving her lips. Triumph and possession flash in her eyes, a glimpse of the monster lurking beneath the veneer of beauty and grace.

Two predators circling each other, ready to strike.

11

Emily

Shadows dance across oak-paneled walls of the parlor as a fire crackles in the fireplace. Plush armchairs and a sofa form a cozy circle, and the familiar faces of my friends come into view as they file in from the patio outside, drinks in hand and laughter on their lips.

Rachel smooths her dress, sinking into the sofa beside Jack with a contented sigh. Her long curls tumble over bare shoulders. I catch Jack watching her, and a surge of anxiety swells up in my stomach.

I glance away and busy myself with stoking the fire. The flames cast a warm glow over the room, chasing away the chill that has crept into my bones.

Sarah and Lucas tumble into an armchair together, a tangle of limbs and giggles, Lucas's glasses askew. Whatever reservations Sarah had about this weekend, seem to have gone out the window. Ava may be the one with the blossoming drinking problem, but

Sarah has a long and storied history of uncharacteristic decisions under the influence. Since our college days, there has been a joke that liquor turns her into someone else entirely. Even she can't deny it.

I try not to judge Sarah and Lucas for being handsy. Sarah had a baby nine months ago, and it's no secret the transition to motherhood hasn't been an easy one for her. I would like to believe that motherhood will come more naturally to me, but I cannot assume that either. Time will tell.

Will was the first to say that Sarah needs this weekend more than anyone, and something tells me he likes this side of her, that he enjoys watching her come out of her shell.

Beside Sarah and Lucas, Ava plunks down in a chair with a huff, downing her drink in one go. Her eyes are foggy, and she spits out snarky words like bullets.

"So, who's up for a little game of musical chairs?" Ava drawls, words dripping with sarcasm. Rachel shoots her an icy glare, but Ava just cackles in response, the sound grating on my nerves. I try not to judge her either; I can't imagine what it would be like to be a widower, especially at her age. Nor can I imagine what it would be like to be here alone, with all of us couples. I know she misses Brian. We all do.

Ava looks at me as though she senses what I'm thinking, so I keep my face neutral and peer into the fire, listening to the trivial chatter and laughter of my friends with half an ear. My thoughts drift back to Will, wondering when he'll make an appearance, and a flush creeps up the back of my neck at the thought.

I know I shouldn't let my mind go there. It's an arrangement born of one too many drinks and bored thirty-somethings. It's absurd, but Rachel posed this as a weekend to shed the masks of our everyday lives, something Jack and I are used to. It's just a silly game, I tell myself.

No one will get hurt.

I cling to that promise like a lifeline, watching the flames dance, waiting.

But the fire does nothing to stop the cold that has taken hold inside me.

I glance up as the door to the parlor creaks open, my heart skipping a beat. Will stands in the doorway, leaning one broad shoulder against the frame, a glass of bourbon cradled in one hand. His eyes find mine from across the room, a slow smile curving his lips, and I feel something inside me shift, as though a part of me rearranges itself to accommodate this new desire.

"There you are," Rachel says, her voice edged with impatience. "Come join us."

Will strides into the room, settling into the armchair beside mine. The spicy scent of his cologne reaches me, and I fight the urge to inhale deeply. Our arms brush as he sits, and a spark of electricity races up my arm at the contact.

"My apologies," Will says, not sounding particularly sorry. His knee presses against mine as he takes a slow sip of his drink, watching me over the rim of the glass.

His gaze feels dangerous, so I stare into the fire, doing my best to ignore his intense presence next to me. My heart slams against my ribcage as the anxiety over what we've arranged, what Jack might have planned, and whether I can trust him, builds.

"Shall we go over the rules again?" Rachel asks, breaking the tension.

I can't help but fidget as I turn to look at Lucas and Sarah. "Maybe we should reconsider," I say.

Rachel's eyebrow arches in skepticism as she directs her gaze toward me. "Are you sure you want to back out now?"

"I'm just tired," I explain with a yawn, "and it seems like you guys are only just getting started. I don't want to be the reason Will loses."

A collective groan echoes in the room. "We get it," Ava sighs. "You're exhausted. You need your beauty sleep."

"Come on now, Rach has planned this getaway for weeks," Lucas says, pouting. "I'll put on a pot of coffee—it's not every day we all get to spend time together."

Guilt floods my chest. "Okay. Fine."

"Good," Rachel says curtly before taking a sip of her drink. "Remember, what happens here stays here," she stresses. "No one will ask about what goes on behind closed doors and if anyone wants to stop, they are free to do so without any hard feelings. There are plenty of rooms available to retreat to if necessary."

Her gaze pins mine, and I give a stiff nod in agreement.

"Does everyone understand?" Rachel presses.

Nods of consent ripple through the group, and satisfaction softens Rachel's features. She lifts her glass, the ice clinking. "To a fun weekend with good friends."

"To a fun weekend," we echo, and the chill slips from my bones, warmth suffusing my limbs as I chance a glance at Will. His eyes crinkle at the corners as we clink glasses, bourbon sloshing over his fingers, and anticipation curls low in my belly.

Later, Will tilts his head toward me, a lock of dark hair falling across his forehead. "So, Emily, Jack's forever complaining that you're always working...but surely you find time for a little R&R every now and again..."

His words hang in the air, heavy with suggestion. I glance away, searching for something safe to say. "I enjoy reading... mainly business books."

"Is that so?" Interest lights his eyes, blue as the ocean stretching beyond the windows. "I'd love to discuss strategies for negotiating acquisitions."

My lips curl into a smile. "I'm always happy to talk shop."

Out of the corner of my eye, I see Rachel laughing at something Jack has said.

"Excellent." Will shifts closer, and I catch another whiff of his cologne, sandalwood and bergamot. "I have to say, I've always thought your success in venture capital is quite inspiring. Not many women make it to the top in that field."

"Years of tenacity and hard work," I say, my pulse skittering under Will's loaded admiration. "It's not for everyone, but the rewards are worth it."

"That I can see," he says, his eyes lingering. "You seem like the type of woman who knows what she wants and won't stop until she gets it."

I take a sip of my bourbon to hide my smile. "Maybe."

The flirtation in Will's tone is unmistakable, his knee nudging against mine, and I find myself leaning into his touch. A new excitement thrums under my skin at the prospect of where the night might lead.

Jack's gaze flickers to us for a moment before he returns his attention to Rachel. I feel my husband pushing me toward this, though I'm not sure why. He couldn't care less about the money, so I know it must be a test. Part of me feels infuriated, the other part hurt and betrayed. We've always tested others, never each other.

I suppose he wants these people out of our lives for good, and he sees this as his golden opportunity. He's trying to prove a point, and so far, it's working in his favor.

An uncomfortable heat rises up my neck as guilt mixed with confusion settles in. But one look at the hunger in Will's eyes erases any doubts, replacing them with a rush of something else. What, exactly, I'm not sure.

The weekend, it seems, will be full of surprises.

12

Emily

A crash rings out, and we spin to see Ava careening through the parlor, an empty glass in her hand. A wave of bourbon splashes against the hardwood floor.

"Whoops!" she titters, barely keeping her balance before she topples over.

Sarah jumps up. "Ava, I think you've had enough."

"Nonsense!" Ava waves away the suggestion, her eyes glassy. She takes a wobbly step forward and knocks into the end table, sending an antique vase plunging to the floor.

Rachel groans, pinching the bridge of her nose. "Ava, sit down before you hurt yourself."

"Why don't you make me?" Ava growls, swaying slightly, with one hand clutching the back of an armchair for support. "It's not like any of you really care, anyway. You don't care about me—or about Brian—or that he's rotting in some grave. All you care about is your stupid little game!"

I stand and reach for her arm. "Ava, stop. You know that's not true, and you don't mean—"

She whirls around, eyes blazing. "Don't touch me! What do you know about thinking clearly? You selfish, heartless bitch!"

I flinch at the venom in her tone, hurt slicing through me. We may have all had too much to drink tonight, but there's no excuse for such language.

"You barely even called after Brian died!" Ava shouts. "Remember? No? Well, I do! And so does everyone else. Your work was too important—"

I want to tell her she's wrong, but the words won't come. We all like to think we'll be there for our friends in a time of need, but life is not exactly that convenient. There was a big deal I was working on, and I couldn't let my team down. If I dropped the ball, it wouldn't have just affected me, it would have impacted everyone. "I—"

Will grips my elbow lightly and shakes his head. "Let it be."

I can't help but feel embarrassed at being called out, and I can see that everyone is waiting for an argument that I don't really want to have.

"Come on," Will says, nodding toward the door. "Let's get some fresh air—it might do us all some good."

I hesitate, torn between the chaos in the parlor and the prospect of escape. In the end, the hurt and anger simmering inside win out. "Yes, fresh air sounds lovely."

Will leads me down the hall and the stairs and then out the large glass doors onto the patio. The crisp night air washes over me, cooling my flushed skin. I take a deep breath, the tension easing from my shoulders.

"I'm sorry about that," Will says. "Ava has had a lot to drink. She didn't mean what she said."

"I know." I shrug, feigning nonchalance. "We've all had a bit too much tonight. Things will look better in the morning."

But as the words leave my lips, I sense this isn't true. The facade is crumbling, fractures threatening to shatter the foundation of our friendship.

Still, I force those worries aside and focus on placing one foot in front of the other as Will guides me along a winding stone path through manicured hedges and topiary, the shadows deepening with each step. I'm sure it's the bourbon and the wine, but a forbidden intimacy bubbles up within me, like my stomach is filled with thousands of fluttering butterflies.

I glance at Will from the corner of my eye, noticing the predatory gleam in his eyes, the hungry set of his mouth. Heat pools in my belly, anticipation quickening my pulse. He's a businessman, and good businessmen can smell weakness a mile away.

When Will stops in front of a marble bench, I'm almost relieved. My heart is galloping, palms sweating profusely. Yet there's the thrill of it, too, an intoxicating mix of trepidation and longing. Suddenly, I miss Jack, and I regret trying to make him jealous.

Will turns to face me, eyes shimmering in the pale moonlight. "Do you trust me, Emily?"

The question catches me off guard, but I do not waver. The truth is, I don't trust anyone, except maybe Jack, but even now I feel misgivings creeping in. "Yes."

A sly grin plays on Will's lips, as though he already knows the truth. He moves quickly, pushing me with a firm hand onto the bench. His body is atop mine before I can make a move. I take in a sharp breath, my hands finding his biceps.

Will's hot breath caresses my ear, sending an electric current from my head to my toes. "Good," he rumbles, relishing in his power over me. "Because we're about to have some real fun."

Fear courses through me as I realize this isn't part of our game. It's too late—Will has me pinned, and under his gaze I'm not putting up half the fight I should be.

"Now," he whispers wickedly, fingers tracing along my thigh. "Which part of you should I break in first?"

13

Emily

I struggle to push Will off. "Not funny."

"No?" he grins. "My apologies," he says, but he doesn't look sorry.

He searches my face and then rolls off me, giving me space to breathe again. I sit up, straightening my dress with trembling hands.

"I didn't mean to scare you," Will says softly. He reaches out to brush a strand of hair from my face. "I just wanted to see if you put your money where your mouth is—if you *really* trust me."

"I wasn't scared," I scoff, fighting to keep my voice steady.

Will sighs as if skeptical but doesn't press me on it. We sink into silence, the only sounds the rustling leaves and waves crashing in the distance. My pulse gradually slows, an odd mix of disappointment and relief swirling inside me.

"I guess there's a part of me that wants to see if you'll tell Jack."

"Why would I?"

"You tell me," he says. "All I know is I'm sick of this stalemate between us."

I don't know if Will is talking about him and my husband or between he and I, and I'm not sure I want to.

After a long moment, Will clears his throat. "It's a beautiful night." His eyes drift to the inky sky, scattered with stars that shine like diamonds on black velvet.

"It is," I agree quietly. My anger fades, and I'm left with a kind of peace that frustrates me, because I don't know what it means or where it's leading me.

Will's eyes meet mine again, pale blue in the silvery light of the moon. "Do you ever wonder if there's something more out there?"

I squint at him, not following the sudden shift in conversation. "More than what?"

"More than this." He gestures vaguely at the garden, the house, the lives we've built. "More than the daily grind and keeping up appearances."

A bitter edge creeps into his tone. "Always wanting something we don't have."

His words strike a chord and I look away, a pang of sorrow piercing my chest. After six years of marriage, there are still moments when I feel adrift in a sea of unfamiliarity with Jack. Perhaps it's the alcohol talking, but I can't help but wonder if we're still on the same page, if we still want the same things.

"We're not the same people anymore," he says.

"I don't know so much about that," I tell him, thinking of Jack, thinking of those peculiar interests of my husband's, of his unyielding desire for justice—I always thought they were a phase, a flash of impulsive whimsy that he would soon relinquish. But now I see I was wrong. This is who Jack is.

Suddenly, Will's hand closes over mine and shakes me out of my reverie, drawing me back to reality. There's something knowing in his eyes that makes me wonder if he can see right through me—if he knows of the cracks in my relationship, the pieces of myself I've sacrificed to maintain the status quo.

A flush of shame washes over me at the intimacy of his touch and I pull away, wrapping my arms around my waist. What am I doing? This is dangerous territory, and I can already feel myself slipping.

"We should go back inside," I say.

Will studies me for a long moment before nodding. "Of course." His lips quirk into a wry smile. "After all, we have a long weekend of pretense ahead of us."

I force a light laugh, though his words strike deeper than I care to admit. "Something like that."

Will stares at me, eyes softening. "Emily, I—"

He stops, shaking his head. "Never mind."

I study him as he stands and offers me his hand. I hesitate, then take it. Will pulls me to my feet and into his arms.

"Dance with me," he whispers, drawing me close.

I don't protest as Will leads me in a slow dance across the garden path. His hand rests on the small of my back, his other entwined with mine. We sway gently to the music of the night, the crickets chirping a lullaby.

Being this close to Will is intoxicating. His cologne, woodsy and masculine, makes my head swim. I close my eyes, leaning into his chest.

"I've wanted this for so long," he breathes in my ear.

My eyes fly open. "What?"

"You." His voice is low, but steady. "I've wanted you since the day we met."

My breath catches in my throat. "But you're married to Sarah."

The words sound impossibly stupid after I say them, and I know they're meaningless, nothing more than semantics, but it's what comes to mind.

"Sarah and I haven't been together in years, not really." Will spins me out, then draws me back close to him. "We're only staying together for the sake of appearances—well, that and the fact she got pregnant."

"You seem so happy." This isn't a lie. Sure, Sarah's dealing with a touch of postpartum depression, but I wouldn't say she and Will are unhappy.

He shakes his head sadly. "I love Ian, but I didn't want to be a dad—not yet, anyway."

I jerk away from him. "Wait—you're serious?"

"I want a divorce, but Sarah won't give me one."

I stare up at Will, stunned. How did I not know this?

"Jack is the same," Will continues. "He doesn't want children, Emily."

"Of course he does." I let go of his hand and take several steps back. "We're actually—we've been trying."

"Jack had a vasectomy years ago."

The ground beneath me shifts.

What is he talking about? Jack doesn't want kids? He had surgery? We've talked about it so many times, made so many plans. It can't be true.

Can it?

"He's been lying to you," Will says softly. "I'm so sorry you had to find out like this. But I can't let you go on believing a lie, either."

My throat tightens, and tears prick at my eyes. How could Jack do this? Did our future together mean nothing at all? He had to know I'd find out eventually. My husband plans every detail; he wouldn't have missed that one.

"How do you know he had a vasectomy?" I say. "Jack told you this?"

"Because I was the one who drove him."

A tsunami of hurt and betrayal crashes over me, threatening to pull me under. Will steps forward, trying to bring me in for a hug. I feel unsteady on my feet, so I let him.

"Shh," he whispers, stroking my hair. "It's going to be okay."

But it's not. Nothing will ever be okay again.

14

Emily

Will and I enter the parlor, its eerie stillness like a noose around my neck. The empty chairs and half-finished drinks only add to the unsettling atmosphere. The fire still crackles in the hearth, its light dancing across the walls.

"Where is everyone?" I ask.

Will shrugs. "Looks like they've all retired for the night."

Ava appears from the hallway, her ebony hair pulled high on her head. She takes a swig from a bottle of wine, her expression is unreadable. "They've all retreated to their rooms, like pathetic little mice."

"Ava—"

"What?" She swings the bottle around wildly, gesturing toward bedrooms. "Jack's with Rachel in the room at the end of the hall. Sarah and Lucas are upstairs on the right." She smirks, her lips curled around the neck of the bottle. "Thought you might want to know."

My hands ball into fists at the mention of Jack and Rachel together. The bitter taste of jealousy and betrayal floods my mouth, and I swallow hard. My eyes narrow, fixating on the door that leads to the room down the hall. Part of me wants to storm in there, to confront Jack, to demand the truth, to put an end to this stupid game and this pointless weekend. The other part wants revenge, wants to see how far he is going to take this, and whether it even matters.

But even as I think the thoughts, I know better. Of course, it matters.

Will places his hand on my arm. "Are you all right?"

"I'm fine," I lie through gritted teeth, my fingernails cutting into my palms. I take a step away from him. My heart thumps erratically, powered by ideas of what Jack could be doing behind those closed doors. "I have to talk to Jack."

"Are you sure that's wise?" Will whispers gently, placing a reassuring hand on my shoulder. "I know how you feel, but maybe it's best to wait until morning before making any rash decisions."

"No way I'm getting any sleep," I assure him.

Will gives me a look. "Em, don't do something you'll regret."

I want to insist that I need answers now, but deep down, I know Will is right. My stomach twists with uncertainty. I'm aware that a knockdown, drag-out fight between Jack and I would not only ruin everyone's weekend, it would almost guarantee this was the last time we ever spent time with these friends again. And as much as Will's revelation has changed everything, I am not yet ready to concede to it literally changing *everything*. I suppose the proper term for what I'm feeling is denial.

"It's a private matter," Will insists. "I think you should wait until you get home to discuss it."

"Yeah," I say, because he's right. Will probably knows my husband better than anyone else, aside from me.

"Come on." He gestures toward the stairs. "Let's have a drink in my room and talk this out. Maybe I can shed some light on things..."

Taking a deep breath, I follow him down the dim corridor, the plush carpet muffling our footsteps. As we approach his bedroom door, I can't shake this feeling, like I'm tiptoeing along the edge of something dangerous.

He pushes open the door, and the moonlight illuminates a luxurious sanctuary. The king-sized bed is draped in silk sheets, and although it is dark, there's a breathtaking view of the ocean. I can hear the waves crashing relentlessly against the shore.

Will pours two drinks, handing me one as he raises an eyebrow. The alcohol warms me from within, and my pulse quickens.

"Nice, huh?" He asks after he takes a sip himself. "Now, about Jack..."

I take a swig of bourbon to steady my nerves. "It doesn't make any sense," I say, looking out the window. "Why would he have surgery without telling me?"

Will leans against the window, sipping his drink thoughtfully. "People do strange things when they're scared, Emily."

"Scared?" I've never known Jack to be scared of anything. It's one of the things I love most about him.

"Maybe he's scared of losing you," Will adds pointedly, his penetrating stare leaving me feeling exposed and vulnerable. "Or maybe he's scared of becoming a father."

His words sting like salt on an open wound, and I swallow hard and look away.

"Either way, you deserve answers."

I give a terse nod, my heart hammering as I take another swig of bourbon, downing my glass in one go. The room crackles with tension, and I'm flooded with an overwhelming sadness.

Will strides over to the liquor cabinet and pours me another drink, pressing it into my hands. The amber liquid burns my throat but does little to soothe the knot in my stomach.

Will sinks onto the sofa, patting the spot beside him. "Come, sit."

I hesitate, then join him. His thigh presses against mine, and I know being here is a terrible idea, but I can't bring myself to care. I take another sip of bourbon, aware of his eyes on me.

"You seem troubled," he says. "Is there something else?"

I want to tell him everything—all the things Jack has done—the things *I've* done. I want to tell him how my heart aches and how I'm terrified it will never be put back together again—but all I can manage is a weak shake of my head. "It's nothing. I'm fine."

"Nonsense. I can see the turmoil in your eyes." He tilts my chin up, forcing me to look at him. His fingers linger on my skin, tracing a line of fire. "You can tell me anything, Emily."

The intensity of his voice, his conviction, it nearly overwhelms me. But this is dangerous ground we're treading, and I know I should make my excuses and leave before things progress beyond the point of no return.

And yet, I find myself saying, "You're right. It's Jack. I don't know what's gotten into him lately. He's become distant, secretive. I worry there's something he's not telling me. Something else."

Will's eyes darken. "I see. I know you're aware of our difficulties…"

His hand slides to the nape of my neck as he starts to massage the tense muscles there. I fight back the urge to moan, feeling my willpower fading with each passing second. "Yeah…"

"Jack is… Well, Jack is *Jack*. And by that, I mean difficult."

"I don't know if I can trust him anymore," I whisper. "Because everything between us feels like a lie."

"You deserve more than that," Will says in a strained voice. His other hand moves to cup my cheek, sending a wave of heat through me. "You deserve to be adored and respected. Not deceived or lied to."

His words pierce my heart, and I force away tears. I've longed to hear these words for so long, and coming from Will rather than Jack almost undoes me.

"Emily, look at me."

I lift my eyes to his, and the desire I see there steals my breath.

"Let me take care of you tonight. No one has to know."

I know I should refuse, but the words die on my lips. I can't deny Will anything in this moment, not when he's offering me the one thing I've been craving.

Comfort. Connection. Passion.

Besides, I'm too drunk anyway. He stands and pulls me to my feet, his hands lingering on my waist. Our bodies are inches apart. The heat radiating from him engulfs me.

"In the garden, you said you trust me…"

I can barely manage a nod.

A smirk crosses his lips. "Then come with me."

He takes my hand and leads me toward the bed, each step filling me with equal parts anticipation and trepidation. My breaths come rapid and shallow. The room is slowly spinning.

Will cradles my face in his hands, his eyes boring into mine. "Relax, Emily. I'm going to take good care of you. For tonight—just let it all go."

His words have an immediate calming effect, and I give a nod in response. He rewards me with a smile.

"Good girl."

My skin flushes at his praise, warmth flooding my extremities. It feels like I'm floating, and while the loss of control feels jarring, I don't hate the sensation. Will softly kisses my lips before traveling along my jaw and down my neck. His hands slide under my dress, gliding up my thighs to grip my hips, and I gasp.

"Will..." My fingers clench onto his shirt, emotion surging through me like a wave—desire and need, warning and regret, all mixed together.

"Shh," he says. "I've got you."

He guides me back until the edge of the bed is pressing against my knees and then, with one strong push, I collapse onto the silk sheets, my heart racing wildly in my chest. This is a mistake. I know it's a mistake. But I do not say no.

Will towers above me, eyes dark with promise. "Now, where were we?"

15

Anonymous

Who knew I had such a penchant for voyeurism? Certainly not me. But when an opportunity presents itself, well, you grab it.

I watch as he drops to his knees beside the bed, hands sliding up her calves to grip behind her knees. He splits her legs and settles between them, gazing up at her through lowered lashes.

"You're so beautiful like this. So willing and pliant under my hands." His fingers trail higher, nudging her dress up to her hips. "I'm going to make you mine, piece by piece, until you're begging for mercy."

I hate every second of this encounter, yet I can't look away.

A whimper escapes her lips at his words. He grins, slow and predatory, before lowering his head. His breath ghosting over the fabric has her squirming, either repelled or desperate for more contact— I can't tell which one.

"Patience," he whispers against the lace. His fingers curl into the sides of her panties and tug them lower with a deliberate slowness that's almost cruel.

He is going to ruin her marriage—ruin her life—but, hey, at least she's enjoying it.

She clenches involuntarily, a nervous heat radiating from every pore on her body as she stares up at him with unspoken need in her eyes.

He chuckles before leaning in to press a kiss to her inner thigh. His tongue slides through her folds without warning, and I watch as silent shockwaves ripple through her body before morphing into pleasure that nearly shatters me with its intensity.

"Please..."

"All in good time, darling."

A fractured moan escapes her lips as he settles into an excruciating rhythm, flicking and sucking until she's writhing against his mouth.

The coil in her belly winds tighter and tighter, pleasure bordering on pain, as he relentlessly drives her higher. She's almost incoherent, submerged in a fog of desire and hunger, when he pulls away.

Her eyes fly open to find him poised above her, lips wet and swollen. "Don't worry, sweetheart. I'm nowhere near done with you."

"I—"

"Relax," he whispers in her ear. His breath feathers across her neck, raising goosebumps. I try to still my trembling hands, worried they can feel the wild pounding of my heart through the camera. My mind knows this is impossible, but my body doesn't seem convinced. "We're just getting to know each other."

One hand slides up to cup her breast through the thin fabric of her dress. She gasps, heat flashing through her. Her nipple hardens under his touch. But I feel nothing. Nothing but pure, white-hot rage.

"Stop," she rasps, and for a moment, it seems like she can sense my hostile energy from far away. *This is a mistake. You will pay.* But she doesn't move away, paralyzed by her own confusion and the waves of pleasure coursing through her veins. Somewhere deep down inside she knows this has gone too far, too fast—but there's some masochistic part of her that wants to see how far he'll push her boundaries. Or rather, how far she'll allow him to push them.

"I don't think that's what you really want," he growls, his fingers teasing her nipple to a rigid peak. She bites her lip against a moan, torn between pleasure and dismay. "Admit it. You like playing with fire."

His words hit home, and it's clear she has no ready answer. She's in over her head, caught in a riptide of lust and poor judgment, and it's pulling her under with terrifying speed. She wants it to stop, but not badly enough to make it happen. I'm not sure what to make of all this, but one thing is certain: This won't end well. I will make sure of it.

16

Emily

Will's fingers slide under the edge of my panties, seeking and finding the source of my arousal. I gasp as he strokes through my folds, my pleasure spiking sharply.

"You're so wet for me already," he whispers against my ear. "Say it. Say you want me to fuck you right here, where anyone could walk in."

I swallow hard, torn between indignation at his crudeness and undeniable desire. I know I should put a stop to this, but the words stick in my throat. I can't seem to summon the effort to push him away, even as this spins out of control.

He plunges two fingers inside me, and I cry out at the invasion, my inner muscles clenching around the intrusion. It's too much, too fast, overloading my senses, but I rock my hips into his hand, chasing the pleasure that threatens to consume me.

"Say it." He thrusts relentlessly into me with a fierce intensity. I ignore his orders, and before long, he has me balancing on the edge of climax, so close I can taste it, but he won't give me release until I admit defeat.

I lick my lips, struggling to form the words. At last, in a rush of breathless surrender, I give him what he wants. "Okay. Fine. Yes. I want you to fuck me."

Victory flashes in his eyes as his expert touch finds the hidden gem that brings forth my shattering release. My orgasm rips through me, leaving me limp and trembling in its wake. Will withdraws his fingers and brings them to his lips, tasting my essence with a sly grin.

"Delicious," he says. "I knew you had it in you. All that restraint and composure, hiding a perfect little slut within." His words should infuriate me, but instead, a traitorous heat blooms under my skin. I grip the bedsheets, still reeling from the intensity of my release, and his teasing only serves to fan the flames.

"Don't worry, darling." He pauses and shakes his head, a smirk playing across his face. "I'll give you everything you need. All you have to do is ask."

My eyes snap shut as his stubble scrapes against my neck, the sensation setting off a chain reaction of pleasure. But I'm not satisfied, not yet. The promise in his voice is enough to fuel my desire further, and all I want to do now is drown in sensation until nothing else matters.

Will kisses a path up to my lips, pushing them apart with his tongue. And it's the taste of myself that drives me wild—the knowledge that he wants me so much that he can't help but take a little bit of me with him everywhere he goes.

Fuck, I'm drunk.

My hands clench at his shirt fiercely, desperate to keep him close. There's no turning back—we're caught up in a stormy sea of lust with no escape except into each other. Any thought of consequence slips away as I surrender to passion and the man who stokes its fire.

Will quickens his pace, slamming into me now, ruthless and

demanding. I meet each thrust eagerly, chasing oblivion, hard and fast, and then—a strangled scream tears from my throat as ecstasy crashes over me in blinding waves. Will follows soon after, his body relaxing on top of mine.

We lie together, spent and gasping for breath, until eventually exhaustion seeps into my limbs, and my eyes flutter shut.

But just before I succumb to sleep, a stray thought drifts through my mind: *What have I done?*

17

Jack

I'm still groggy as I rush into the kitchen, my heart pounding in sync with the blood pulsing through my veins. The smell of iron assaults me as I take in the gruesome sight—Will's dead body draped on the cold pantry floor, his wide eyes staring on, frozen in shock. His dark hair is soaked with blood and forms a macabre halo around his head. A knife protrudes from his neck like something from a cheesy horror movie.

I run my hand across my jaw. "Jesus Christ."

Emily barges past me, her face ashen with terror. She looks like she's about to be sick, and I can't blame her.

"Is he...?" Her voice fades away, scared to vocalize the awful truth.

"Dead," I confirm.

The chef clears his throat. I notice his hands shaking as he backs away from the body. "I found him like this."

I tried to tell Emily about hired help. Almost no one is trustworthy nowadays, but she didn't listen. Now, she's saying something ludicrous. Something that sounds like she wants me to check for a pulse again, as though I'm an idiot, as though neither of us has seen a dead body before.

A chorus of gasps, sobs, and hushed whispers instantly fill the kitchen as Sarah crumples to the ground in grief. Emily's green eyes cloud over with guilt and something else—paranoia, plain and simple. I can see the gears turning in her head—she knows that what happened last night could very well have led to this. She just stands frozen in place, staring at Will's corpse with an intensity that makes my stomach churn.

The oppressive air in the room presses down on me like a suffocating weight. I'm the only one who can take charge; there's nobody else to rely on.

"Michael," I say, nodding to the phone in the corner. "Call the police."

He hesitates, eyes on Will's lifeless body, then pulls out his cell phone.

Emily's voice is tight with fear. "Jack, what are we gonna do?"

"Listen," I tell her, pulling her close so no one else can hear. "We have to keep quiet about where we were last night and who we were with. Nobody needs to know."

"Are you sure?" she asks, her voice trembling. "If we're caught in a lie—"

"I'm aware." I grip her hand tightly. "But we need to protect ourselves."

Reluctantly, she nods, squeezing my hand in return. We exchange a tense glance before refocusing on the others.

I consider the best way to make sure everyone gets the message without making myself look suspicious. Thankfully, luck is on my side and I don't have to because Lucas clears his throat, garnering everyone's attention. "All right," he says, forcing a semblance of authority into his voice. "We're going to stick to a simple story: we were all here, enjoying a weekend away, and then this happened. Nobody mentions the swap. Understood?"

They all nod, their faces pale and drawn. Sarah sniffles, wiping her cheeks with the back of her hand. Michael hangs up the phone, his expression grim.

Chaos erupts around us as Emily frantically paces back and forth like a caged animal. I watch her, concerned and conflicted. Her guilt is palpable, feeding off itself like a snake devouring its own tail.

"Jack," she says, halting abruptly and staring straight at me. "I didn't do this."

"Of course not." I try to sound reassuring. But there's no denying the small, dark part of me that wonders if this is one of my wife's many games.

She glowers. "Then who did? And why?"

"Maybe it was..." My voice fades away as I search for a credible explanation, but my words are drowned by the growing wail of sirens. They're getting closer, and Emily's panic intensifies with every passing second.

"Jack," she shrieks, digging her nails into my arm like sharp claws. "We need to get our story straight. I can't let them find out about..."

Her eyes dart toward Will's deceased body, her cheeks reddening with a concoction of remorse and thrill.

"About what, Em?" I ask, gritting my teeth against the pain in my arm.

Fresh tears cascade down her face. "That I was with him."

She swallows hard. "I mean, nothing happened. But we were, you know, together. I was the last person to see him—"

"Got it," I say, cutting her off. "We'll figure it out. But right now, we need to concentrate on getting through the next few minutes."

"I know. But..." She releases her grip on my arm. The marks she leaves behind are deep and red, a stark contrast against my skin. "Jack," she says again, her voice strained. "I can't help but feel like we're making a huge mistake."

"We don't have a choice."

"It's just—"

"Em, it's better if you don't say anything."

She looks away from me, her eyes cast downward. I don't miss the slight nod as she acknowledges the truth of what I've said. "It's going to be okay," I assure her. "It always is."

As sirens sound in the distance and police cars start to pull up outside, I take one final look at Will's body. The blood pooling around him is dark and thick, like molasses, and I can't help but feel a perverse relief at the sight. I didn't kill him, but I'm not the least bit sorry he's dead.

I prepare to face the incoming storm. "You good?"

Emily nods, her eyes filled with determination and something darker, something that both excites and terrifies me.

As car doors slam, we brace ourselves for the questions, the accusations, the twisted games that are sure to follow. And as I stand there, shoulder to shoulder with my beautiful, treacherous wife, I can't help but think: what the hell have we gotten ourselves into?

18

Emily

Everything is a blur. There's a chaotic movie scene playing out before me—the world in slow motion, each frame smeared with fingerprints of confusion and doubt.

The sun beats down, burning the back of my neck as police officers swarm the mansion like ants at a picnic. Their uniforms, a stark contrast to the idyllic setting, cling to their bodies, damp with sweat. They secure the area with yellow crime scene tape, a vibrant ribbon cutting through nature's serenity.

A tall figure separates himself from the hive of activity, his polished shoes reflecting the sunlight as he approaches us. He introduces himself as Detective Alvarez. The man seems stitched together from darkness itself, his ebony hair slicked back and his obsidian eyes scanning the area with unnerving precision.

He studies his phone quickly before looking directly at Jack, then at me. His gaze pierces my soul, as though he can read everything that I'm thinking—everything that I've done. "I'm here to find out what happened to your friend," he says.

"Will," I whisper, my voice cracking against the oppressive heat. My heart hammers against my ribs in desperate tempo. "His name is Will."

"Will, yes." He takes our faces into account, as if one of us will break under the weight of his harsh stare. "I'm sorry for your loss. Shall we go inside?"

We move silently into the house, lingering about the living room without words or purpose, all while Sarah's sobs echo around us. She has just broken the news to her mother about what happened to Will. She needs to call Will's mother next.

Alvarez narrows his eyes. "Let's start with what happened last night."

"It was pretty uneventful," Jack answers, crossing his arms defensively. "We had dinner, played some games, went to bed. Just a normal weekend among friends."

"Nothing like the kind we used to have," Rachel adds. "When we were young."

"Really?" Detective Alvarez raises an eyebrow, skepticism dripping from the word. "Normal weekends among friends don't usually end with dead bodies."

"Detective, we're just as shocked as you are," Ava insists, her voice trembling. She wrings her hands together. "None of us wanted this."

"Of course not," Alvarez concedes, staring at his phone. "But someone did, and I intend to find out who."

Alvarez tosses his phone onto the coffee table and sighs. "We'll need to speak with each of you separately, so hang tight."

Rachel shifts uncomfortably. "How long is this gonna take? We have spa appointments—that, uh, I need to cancel."

"A few hours, I'd guess. Maybe a little more," Detective Alvarez says. "I wouldn't make plans for a while. And if you haven't alerted the rental company already, I suggest you do so now."

"Great." Ava throws her hands up. "As if this weekend couldn't get any worse. Now, we're stuck in this cursed house for God knows how long."

"Cheer up," Alvarez says. "At least you're still alive."

He turns toward me, his pen hovering over his notepad. I don't know if I'm relieved or petrified that he's starting with Jack and me, but I do my best to keep my heart from exploding out of my chest. "Let's get some basic information from each of you."

I hand him my driver's license, then quickly scan the room, taking in the expressions of my friends. This weekend was supposed to be a fun getaway for us all, but now it feels like a trap. "None of this makes any sense."

Detective Alvarez ignores me and with a wave, his team springs into action. They move with the precision of a well-oiled machine. One officer snaps photos of the crime scene while another is combing the layout of the first floor. A third officer, carrying an evidence collection kit, begins dusting for fingerprints.

Meanwhile, Alvarez peppers us with questions. It feels like hours, *days*, sitting there under the scrutiny of his glare. We do our best to answer them, and I suppose we pass the test, because eventually he moves on and neither of us ends up in handcuffs.

Hours pass. Finally, the detective moves to the center of the room and clears his throat.

"All right, listen up," he says addressing the group. "It's likely we'll have additional questions in the days to come. Should we need to interview you further—we'll contact you to schedule a time. In the meantime, I'm leaving each of you with my card should anything come to mind that may help with the investigation."

The thought of being interrogated sickens me, but I nod along with the others, resigned to our fate. It's clear we're all suspects in Will's murder, and none of us can escape the probing eyes of the law.

"Until then," he continues, "I suggest you all go home and get some rest. We'll be in touch."

We exchange nervous glances, and the silence stretches out between us, heavy and suffocating. It feels like no one will ever break it.

"I'll gather our things," Jack says, the words bitter on his tongue. He turns and stalks away, slamming the door behind him as he leaves. The sudden noise jolts me, and I rub my arms, trying to ward off the chill creeping up my neck.

"The rental company wants us out," Rachel says. "Obviously."

Ava's eyes scan the group. "No way I'd stay in this house another night."

One by one, the rest of us disperses, each person retreating into their own private world of grief and despair. Lucas casts a last, lost look around the room before slinking away. Rachel marches out, her chin held high, refusing to give anyone the satisfaction of seeing her rattled. Sarah wavers for a moment, her eyes meeting mine, and then she too disappears, leaving only Ava and me behind.

We stand there in silence until Jack returns, bags in hand. "Does Sarah have a ride?"

"Lucas and Rach are driving her to her mom's."

Jack nods and then shoots a look at Ava. "And you? Need a ride or anything?"

"I'm fine. I packed up last night. I was planning to head home then, but Rachel took my keys." She glances toward the front door. "What a mistake that was, staying."

"You'd had a lot to drink," Jack says, stating the obvious. "We have one friend to bury. We don't need another."

"Fuck off." Ava shakes her head and then storms out. I call after her, but Jack grabs my arm, and I know it's futile.

I look at him and sigh heavily. "But did you really have to say that?"

"What? It's the truth." He thrusts my bag in my direction. "Let's get the hell out of here."

As I follow him outside, the humidity hits me in the face, but it does little to clear my head. My thoughts are a tangled mess of confusion and fear, and I can't shake the feeling that something evil has wormed its way into our lives. With each step I take, the weight grows heavier on my shoulders.

I glance back at the house, an imposing figure looming against the bright sky. It's hard to believe that just yesterday we were all laughing and enjoying ourselves, blissfully unaware of the storm that was about to descend upon us. Now, our lives have been irrevocably changed, and there's no going back.

As I trudge up the drive to the car, the wind whispers through the trees, carrying with it a chilling question: Which one of us is capable of murder? And more importantly, is it going to stop with Will?

19

Jack

As in many marriages, my wife and I often remember certain details differently. But with a newfound murder investigation on our hands, it is clear this is going to be much more of an issue than usual.

I peer through the rearview mirror as I press the pedal to the floor. Every second that passes is another step away from it all. Mind racing, I replay every detail in my head, desperately hoping nothing I said will bring our house of cards crashing down.

The second Detective Alvarez stepped through the door, his beady eyes settled on Will's lifeless body, and I knew this was not going anywhere good. From the set of his jaw, it was clear that this case meant something to him—more than just some passing job for a paycheck. He exuded the aura of a man whose identity was deeply entrenched in his work.

"Morning," he said as he fished through his pocket for a pen and notepad. He flashed us a brief smile, and I noticed a gold band adorning his ring finger. "I'm Detective Alvarez. I'll be leading this investigation."

"Jack," I stated firmly, though my heart thundered in my chest. "This is my wife, Emily." Alvarez wrote down our names like it was nothing major. "Nice to meet you. Unfortunate, though, the circumstances."

He slowly raised his gaze to Emily, his eyebrows arched in curiosity. "You two were close to the deceased?"

"Will was—" Emily began, but her voice cracked, betraying her emotions. Tears filled her eyes as she struggled for words.

"Will was a friend," I finished for her, my hand resting on her shoulder. She jerked away with fear-filled eyes that betrayed her guilt. What is she hiding?

"Can you tell me what happened?" Alvarez asked, his pen poised above the notepad.

"Umm," Emily stammered, pacing back and forth as she tried to form a coherent answer. Her eyes darted around the room, her heart no doubt racing, just like mine. "We, uh, we found him like that. In the pantry. Well, Michael found him…"

"Anyone else in the house?" Alvarez inquired, a hint of curiosity on his face. "Besides the seven of you? And the chef?"

"Not that we know of," I said, watching Emily. She looked unwell—still does—her face pale and drained of all its color.

"All right," Alvarez responded gruffly before continuing. "When was the last time either of you saw Will alive?"

"Last night," Emily blurted out, her chest heaving as she stopped pacing. She glared at me, but I could see the fear behind her anger. "We were all together—"

I took her hand and led her over to the couch, asking her to sit.

"—in the parlor," she continued, swallowing hard. "We had some drinks…played some games."

Alvarez narrowed his eyes, scribbling something on his notepad. "Games?"

"Charades," I chimed in, trying to keep my voice steady. The memory of Emily and Will exchanging heated looks in the parlor flashed through my mind. My hands clenched into fists as I fought to suppress the rage.

"Interesting," Alvarez noted. "And after the game?"

"Everyone went to bed," Emily said, her gaze flickering to me for a moment. I could see she was looking for my approval, so I began patting her back in support.

"Copy that," Alvarez said, scribbling some notes in his notepad before turning back to us. "I'll chat with the other parties first, but for now, why don't you both stay put and try to relax? No need to worry." He looked at my wife. "We'll sort this out."

"Thank you, Detective." I forced a smile and watched as he walked away to question the others.

The moment Alvarez was out of earshot, Emily rounded on me.

"What the hell, Jack? You just sat there and said nothing! You let me do all the talking."

"That's not true," I defended myself. "I answered whatever question he asked."

Emily's eyes darted around the room as if someone might be listening in on us. "But you didn't have to mention charades."

Confusion etched itself on my face. "Why does it matter?"

"Because." Venom dripped from her voice. "It's specific. What if the others say something else?"

"You slept with him," I said, not wanting to admit that she was right. I slipped up, but that wasn't at the forefront of my mind. A wave of jealousy crashed over me like an icy wind.

Emily tossed her head back in disbelief. "How can you accuse me of that? Can we just focus on finding out who killed Will instead of playing the blame game?"

I let out a deep sigh, accepting her argument—I knew there'd be time for finger pointing later. "All right," I said finally. "But if there's anything you're not telling me, now's the time to come clean."

Emily bit her lip and then looked away. "There's nothing else," she whispered, but I could tell she was lying.

I've let it go for now, but I'll damn sure be keeping an eye on her. We are all suspects in this investigation, and clearly nobody can be trusted completely, not even my own wife.

20

Anonymous

I consider murder to be rather laborious, in the literal sense. Blue collar work. Not the kind I'm fond of, that's for sure, but sometimes it has to be done for the greater good. It's one of those things like working out, or going to the dentist—you know it's important and usually you feel better for having done it. But man is the lead-up to it mind numbing.

So I rolled up my sleeves and got to work. He never should have put his hands on her. I could see it was more than lust, more than a casual passing whimsy, and, well, no. I couldn't stand for it. Did he know he was going to die? Not at first. He fought, though not much. I'm not exactly an amateur—but did I mean to leave the knife in his neck? Also no.

As I stood over his lifeless body, the full weight of my actions hit me. I had taken a life. It didn't matter that it was justified; murder was still murder. Panic began to set in as I frantically searched for any evidence that could be traced back to me. I had been so careful, wearing gloves and a mask, but there was always a chance that something could have been missed.

I gulped down a breath, my stomach churning at the finality of it all. But before I could leave, an eerie sensation came over me. It felt like someone or something was watching me from the shadows.

I couldn't shake the feeling that something terrible was about to happen. I hurried out of the room and made my way down the hallway, but the feeling only grew stronger with each step.

When I reached the bedroom door, I hesitated and looked down the hall. The darkness seemed alive with an unholy presence, and I knew that if I didn't get out of there soon, it would be too late.

My hands were trembling as I opened the door and closed it behind me. Just before I turned around, a figure caught my eye at the bottom of the stairs. It was too dark to make out any details, but I knew one thing—I wasn't alone.

21

Emily

Blood. It's always blood, isn't it? I scrub at the speck on my shirt, never more eager to get home, to strip out of these clothes, and shower.

The weekend getaway that was supposed to be fun and flirty has turned into a nightmare, the kind that leaves you questioning everything you thought you knew about your life. Will is dead. Jack and I are left to pick up the pieces. Sure, we've killed people before—morally corrupt individuals who deserved their fate, or so we told ourselves—but this feels different. The guilt and confusion seep through my veins like a poison I can't escape. I didn't kill him, and yet, I can't help feel like I'm the reason he's dead.

Miles tick by. The air inside the car grows as thick and oppressive as our silence. The smell of leather and tension mingles with the faint traces of cologne that cling to Jack's skin like a desperate lover. I glance at him, his eyes fixed on the winding road ahead, jaw tight enough to shatter.

His fists clench the steering wheel, a testament to the storm brewing beneath the surface.

Outside, the once idyllic landscape now feels all wrong; the trees form a dark, impenetrable wall that seems to close in on us, suffocating any hope for escape. An erratic pulse thunders through my chest, matching the uneven rhythm of the tires over the asphalt.

"Will told me something interesting," I say, shattering the silence with the force of a sledgehammer. "About your *vasectomy*."

Jack's grip tightens, his eyes narrowing. "What did he tell you?"

"Did he need to say more?"

I cross my arms, leaning back against the window as it vibrates with every bump in the road. "You didn't think the procedure you had was important to mention before we started planning for a family?"

"We weren't even talking about kids back then," he says with a sigh. "It was a long time ago."

"A long time ago?" I shift in my seat. "Huh. Regardless—it just seems to me like something you'd mention to the person you're in a relationship with…"

"Oh yeah?" He glances over at me, brows raised. "You know what else seems like something you should mention?"

My heart races as I ask, "What?"

His lips pressed into a grimace. "That you fucked someone else."

The words burst from him like gunfire, his face twisted in accusation. "Is that how he got you into bed? With his brilliant revelations?"

His arrogance infuriates me. "When are you going to admit you killed Will because you were jealous?"

"Jealous?" He scoffs, his grip on the wheel not loosening. "You think I'd kill someone out of jealousy?"

"Let me get this straight—Will told me about your snip job— which you have been lying to me about for *years*," I say, swallowing the lump in my throat. "And instead of admitting it, you accuse me of sleeping with him during the swap? It's like you're trying to frame me...or test me—which, I'm not sure."

"Test you?" Jack's laugh is sharp and bitter, cold as ice. "You're losing it, Emily. Absolutely losing it."

"Am I?" My head whips in his direction. I'm furious at his dismissal. It's so typical of men to play the crazy card. "You want to talk about crazy? You've always been secretive, Jack. You hide behind that enigmatic mask of yours, always leaving me guessing at your true intentions."

"Maybe I have my reasons," he says. "But if you think I'd kill Will just because he told you I had a vasectomy, you don't know me at all."

"Maybe I don't!" Tears roll down my cheeks as I yell at him. "Maybe I never have—but what I do know is that you've killed for less."

"Fine," he snaps. "You want the truth? You think you can handle it?"

I steel myself for whatever revelation he has in store. "Go on."

"Will was going to expose us, Emily."

The words hang heavy in the air, like the final nail in the coffin. "He knew about our past, and he was going to go to the cops."

I stare at him, unable to speak or breathe or even think. My heart pounds in my chest, a relentless drumbeat of fear and betrayal. If Jack is telling the truth, this is worse than I thought, and that's saying a lot because things look bad enough already.

But if he's lying, what else is he capable of?

"I didn't kill him," he says. "But I was planning on it. He was extorting us, Em."

Jack's voice cracks with impatience. "Say something."

I can tell my husband thinks I knew. He thinks I was handling it, and suddenly I feel incredibly stupid. "I don't want to talk about it anymore."

He looks at me with annoyance. "You don't want to talk about it?"

"Drive!" I shout, staring straight ahead, the road stretching into darkness. "Just...drive."

The silence returns, oppressive and unyielding, each mile pulling us further apart. As the evening swallows us whole, I can't help but wonder if there's any way back from this.

22

Jack

The front door groans open, casting an ominous gloom upon the room. Shadows loom and sway across the walls, a physical manifestation of the darkness that threatens to engulf us. Emily flings her bags to one side and kicks off her shoes in a resigned manner. She drifts around the room like a ghost, avoiding my gaze, as if it holds some kind of horrible truth she can't face.

But the fact is, she knows what she's done, and I know it too. For now, that's enough.

Emily trails her fingers over the cool surface of the marble fireplace, but it's a hollow gesture. She's here, but she's not really here—caught in a purgatory of her own making. I watch her, feeling nothing at all.

"Em," I say, my voice catching on the syllables of her name, "we're going to have to talk about this."

Her eyes flicker to mine, a spark of defiance flaring briefly before it dies away. She shrugs. "What's there to say?"

"A lot."

She shakes her head. "Will's dead. We're under investigation. I guess there's not much we can do about it now, is there?"

Her words are laced with bitterness, each one feels like a razor-sharp blade slicing through our fragile marriage.

A distant memory flashes through my mind. I'm back in college, feeling the heat of the frat house basement where I first met Emily, me telling her about some jerk spiking the punch. Her eyes had glittered with dark mischief as she concocted a sinister plan, sealing our fates together with the intoxicating scent of revenge. How could something so beautiful turn into this twisted mess?

The recollection catches me off guard. "It doesn't have to be like this, Em."

"It *is* like this, though, isn't it?"

"You remember how it was when we met?" I ask with a heavy sigh. "Back when we were young and foolish enough to believe that love could conquer all?"

Her eyes narrow with a mixture of bitterness and nostalgia. She knows where I'm going with this. She always knows. "Ah, yes," she sneers, "our college days, when life seemed so simple, and our biggest concern was getting revenge on those who wronged us."

"Exactly." Again, my mind drifts back to that fateful night, our first meeting at the crowded frat party. I can still feel the heat of her breath against my ear as we conspired together, her wicked plan sparking a fire between us that would become an inferno.

The party was raging. Beer kegs and questionable gelatin shots lined the walls as sweat mixed with the smell of weed, the low thumping of bass reverberating off the walls.

The guy in charge of the frat was Brad, notorious for taking advantage of naive girls, plying them with spiked punch he made himself. I wanted to take him down but had to play it careful—there was no room for error.

And then she caught my eye.

Emily stood in a corner, her long brown hair cascading down her back in a white T-shirt and jeans. There was an aura of intelligence and mystery around her, and I was captivated.

I approached her, starting a conversation. At first, she was guarded, but soon her walls crumbled, and we talked like old friends. Her intellect amazed me, feeling like I had finally found someone who could match my wit. Up to that point, most of the girls I dated were surface level. What you saw was what you got. I appreciated that, but I was also very bored and feeling jaded by the status quo.

Emily pointed at Brad, who was busy trying to sweet-talk a girl into drinking his spiked punch.

"We should do something about him," she said.

I stared at her, intrigued.

As Emily described her diabolical plan, meticulously thought out down to the smallest details. I was shocked, yet impressed by her ingenuity. She knew she had to execute her plan without getting caught. That was the most important part. *Not too many witnesses, plenty of suspects.*

We talked throughout the night, and it felt as though I had known Emily my entire life. I was drawn to her darkness, her willingness to take matters into her own hands and seek justice where it was due. It was just a conversation, but I found myself falling for her, and I sensed she felt the same way.

Around three in the morning, we set the plan in motion, flawlessly executing each step. Brad eagerly followed Emily to the rooftop, enticed by the prospect of sharing a joint with a beautiful woman. Oblivious to the unfolding events, he never suspected that he would become a victim of his own demise. With no witnesses in sight, Emily made her ultimate move, pushing him off the roof, watching gravity do its job.

I watched from below as Brad met his seemingly accidental death. A strange mix of satisfaction and relief washed over me.

I knew that was just the beginning. It laid the foundation for our relationship, and I knew keenly that I had found something extraordinary with Emily. She was my partner in crime, someone who saw the world the way I did, someone I could trust. It was love at first sight, or perhaps more accurately, love at first murder.

"That's just it, Jack," Emily says, pulling me back to the present moment. Suddenly, I'm back in our living room looking at my furious wife. "You're still *that* guy. The rest of us grew up."

23

Emily

We stand there, rooted in place, the tension between us palpable. I can feel it coiling around us, binding us together like a twisted lifeline. My mind races, replaying the events of the weekend, searching for answers that remain just out of reach. Jack had every reason to kill Will, but I can't understand why won't he admit it? Is it because it was ill planned? Is he trying to get back at me? I don't know. But I accused him of being childish, which he is.

When I look at him, his eyes are fixed on the floor. "Emily, you know that isn't true."

"Really?" I snap, bitterness lacing my words. "Okay, then, let's start with how you insisted we participate in that godforsaken swap?"

"Look, I never imagined things would go this far." His eyes finally meet mine. "But what's done is done, whether we like it or not."

"Is that right?" I cross my arms over my chest. "Because I feel you're just saying that to save your own skin."

"Emily, please," he says, taking a step toward me. I recoil instinctively, unable to hide the uneasiness that courses through my veins. "I think you're overreacting."

I laugh because my husband has always fancied himself a smart man. And yet, he says the one thing you're never supposed to say to a woman. "You're not thinking logically, Em."

"Fine. Tell me, *how* am I thinking?"

"It's almost like you don't trust me. Which is crazy considering you're the one who slept with someone else—and enemy number one, at that."

"Trust?" I repeat, my laughter hollow and bitter. "How am I supposed to trust you, Jack? After everything that's happened?"

"Because I didn't do it," he says, his voice firm and unyielding. "I didn't kill Will."

"Then who did?" I demand, my voice cracking under the weight of my desperation. "If it wasn't you, then who was it? Sarah? Lucas? Rachel?"

"Maybe," he concedes, his hand rubbing the back of his neck. "Or maybe it was someone else entirely. But the point is, it happened. Will is dead. And like it or not, you giving me the silent treatment will not help our situation."

"Is that supposed to comfort me?"

"Emily..."

The silence between us stretches into an unbearable eternity, broken only by the ticking of the clock on the wall.

Suddenly, a knot forms in my stomach. "How about we talk about what happened between you and Rachel, because I sure as hell know it was something. She could hardly look at me, Jack!"

"You want to know what happened with Rachel?" he asks. "Someone drugged me last night. And if it wasn't you—I suspect it was her."

My eyes widen. "Why would someone drug you? Why would *Rachel* drug you?"

"Maybe to make sure I wouldn't interfere with whatever happened to Will…or maybe I should say *between* you and Will."

His voice is heavy with insinuation, the unspoken accusation hanging in the air between us.

My anger flares, frustration gnawing at my bones like a rabid dog. "You're fucking insane."

"Me?" He gestures wildly at his chest. "You're the one who let that low-life scum fuck you."

With that, I turn away from him and stride across our living room; the walls lined with smart technology that now feels like an electronic prison. The irony of our extravagant surroundings mocking us in our despair isn't lost on me. I storm toward the door, but something stops me—a whisper of impending doom that lingers in the air, making me question whether walking away is truly the answer or if I'll regret it later.

"Don't walk away from me, Em…" Jack's voice trails off, as if he too senses that we've reached a precipice, one that could lead to our salvation or our destruction.

"You don't really want to do that, trust me."

"Isn't it what we both want?" I glance over my shoulder, meeting his eyes. "Freedom. Not to be tied down…certainly not a *family*."

"Be careful what you wish for," he warns me, his voice dark and steady. "You might just get it."

The conviction in his eyes shouldn't surprise me, but it does. I reach for the doorknob. "Then so be it."

As I move to unlock the door, there's a loud pounding on the other side. My eyes immediately find Jack's, and I stand frozen in place.

24

Emily

My hand trembles on the cold brass doorknob as a sudden pounding startles me.

Who could it be at this hour? Through the frosted glass, a blurred silhouette comes into focus.

Rachel.

I swing open the door, my stomach twisting into knots. "Em, I've been trying to reach you all night. Are you okay?" Her eyes are puffy and red-rimmed, mascara streaked under her eyes.

"I'm fine." The lie slips out so easily. "Come in."

Rachel steps inside, rubbing her arms against the chill. "Lucas and I just left Sarah's house. It was horrible, Em—seeing her that way."

"I can only imagine." Guilt gnaws at my insides. I should have been there for my best friend, but the fact that I slept with her husband makes things a little tricky. "I'm going over tomorrow."

"That's good. She really needs her friends right now." Rachel lowers her voice. "Will's dad was there, too. He seems to think Will was into some shady business deals before he died."

Jack's head jerks up, eyes narrowing. My stomach lurches at the implication. Does Rachel suspect? No, not Rachel. She would never—

"Anyway," Rachel continues, "it was all pretty intense. Ava and Sarah were at each other's throats, as usual. You would think they're trying to win some sort of award for who can be the best widow." She sighs, pushing a strand of hair behind her ear. "I'm really worried about her, Em. She's not in a good place."

"I know." I stare at the floor, unsure whether she's speaking of Ava or of Sarah, but it might as well be both.

"It was good of you to invite me in." Rachel's hand closes over mine, her skin soft and warm. "How are you?"

"Excuse me," Jack says before taking the stairs two at a time. Rachel and I both watch as he goes. I study her expression, and suddenly I feel ridiculous for ever thinking anything could happen between her and my husband. Rachel is not, nor has ever been, Jack's biggest fan. And though she may not realize it, the feeling is mutual.

"I'm okay," I say. "Just tired and still in shock."

"Yeah, me too. I'm always here if you want to talk, you know that, right?"

I meet her gaze, struck by the depth of caring in her eyes. Rachel, who has been by my side through heartbreak and loss and all the ups and downs of the past twenty years. Besides Sarah, she's my oldest, dearest friend.

If only she knew the truth.

"I know," I whisper. "Thank you, Rach. For everything."

Rachel smiles, giving my hand a gentle squeeze before letting go. "You're welcome. I just wanted to make sure you were okay." Her eyes flick briefly toward the stairs before settling on me again. "Are things any better with Jack?"

I had confided in Rachel before the getaway that I was

concerned about my husband. He's been antsy since he sold his company, almost jumpy, as if he doesn't quite know what to do with himself. But if Jack is telling the truth about Will's extortion, now I know why.

"Em?"

I hesitate, unsure of how to answer. Are things better? Worse? Irreparably broken? "Yeah, they're better. I mean, all things considered."

Jack chooses that moment to descend the stairs, his footsteps heavy on the wood. My heart leaps at the sight of him in a way that has nothing to do with fear or anger—and everything to do with the way I've felt about him.

"Sorry about that." Jack's tone is smooth as glass as he comes to stand beside me. I feel the warmth of his hand on my lower back, and although I am furious with him, it ignites sparks along my skin.

Rachel's smile tightens. "And you?" she says to Jack. "How are you?"

"Worried," he says and leaves it at that.

An awkward silence follows, broken only by the hum of the air conditioner. I clear my throat, acutely aware of Jack's touch and the conflicting emotions it stirs.

Rachel sighs. "Like I was saying, Will's father was there, going on about how Will was mixed up in some kind of illegal business. He's convinced this is why Will was murdered."

"I feel for Sarah," Jack says, withdrawing his hand. The loss of contact leaves me strangely bereft. "She has a lot on her plate."

Jack crosses the room and leans against the fireplace. I realize he's trying to stir guilt within me. He has the knife in my back, now he's twisting. It should bother me, but instead it turns me on. The tension in the room has reached a fever pitch. I risk a glance in his direction, pulse racing as our eyes meet. His gaze drops to my mouth and lingers there, awakening a slow burn of desire.

My traitorous body remembers all too well the pleasure he can give. But I haven't forgotten the turmoil between us, and I give him a look full of warning, reminding him there are things he could say that he can't take back.

Still, Jack's expression remains unreadable. "That's awful," I say. "I told Sarah I'd stop by tomorrow to see if there's anything she needs."

Rachel nods. "She could really use the support right now. Especially with the baby."

Guilt twists in my gut as I think of Will and Sarah's child. He'll never know his father.

I push the thought away, shaking my head. "I just can't believe he's gone."

"I know," Rachel says softly. "It doesn't seem real."

She looks at me, fear laced in her eyes. "I just get the feeling it could have been any of us."

"It does feel random," I lie.

"Other than what Will's dad said, yeah," Rachel admits. "I just feel so bad for Sarah. I can't stop thinking about her…"

I nod, memories of Sarah and me as kids flooding back. We were always together, giggling over boys, sharing secrets. Sarah was there for me when my parents split up, and again after my brother died. She's always been my rock. Or she had been until Ian was born, and then Sarah changed. But I suppose that is to be expected.

"Sarah's the strongest person I know," I say. "She'll get through this. We'll all help her."

"Of course we will." Rachel smiles, but it doesn't quite reach her eyes. I can see the sadness radiating off her as she stands, smoothing her skirt. "I should head home. Lucas will wonder where I am."

"Tell him to call me," Jack says. He hasn't moved from his spot by the fireplace. His gaze follows Rachel as she makes her way to the front door.

BLOOD, SWEAT, AND DESIRE: A PSYCHOLOGICAL THRILLER

"Thanks for stopping by," I say, walking Rachel out. "I'm glad you came."

"Me too." Rachel hugs me, her perfume enveloping me in a cloud of jasmine and sandalwood. "Call me if you need anything. And let me know how Sarah's doing tomorrow, okay?"

"I will." I close the door behind her with a heavy sigh. When I turn back to the living room, Jack is staring at the floor, lost in thought.

"What are you thinking?" I ask softly.

He shrugs. "Just a lot to process."

I move to stand beside him, slipping an arm around his waist. We stand there for a long moment in silence. The gesture is not exactly an apology, but it's the best I can do.

"Do you really think it could have been anyone?"

"Hard to say." Jack gazes down at me, his blue eyes guarded. "But I have a feeling there's more to this than we know."

"Like what?" I prompt.

Instead of answering, Jack pulls me closer, his lips finding mine, and I realize we're going to solve this the way we solve everything. The way we've *always* solved things.

I melt into the kiss, forgetting my questions, forgetting our argument, forgetting everything. By the time we break apart, I no longer care about Will or his murder, or that I slept with him. I was hurt and drunk. Not that it excuses it, but Jack is not exactly innocent.

But in this moment, none of that matters. All that matters is Jack, and the desire burning between us.

We stumble toward the bedroom, shedding clothes along the way. By the time we reach the bed, we're both naked and breathless with need.

Jack lowers me onto the mattress, his body covering mine. I wrap my legs around his waist, urging him closer. He enters me in one smooth thrust, filling me so completely I cry out.

"Emily." He moves, slow and deep. "You really fucked up."

His words send a thrill through me. "I know," I whisper.

"The question is what to do about it…"

"Do whatever you want."

Jack groans, increasing his pace. The bed creaks under us, my gasps and cries mingling with the sound of flesh on flesh.

"Look at me," he commands. I open my eyes to find him gazing down at me, pupils blown wide with lust and something more primal. Possession. "If you betray me again, it will be the last time you lie to anyone ever again."

"I know."

With a roar, Jack shudders his release. The feel of him pulsing inside me sends me tumbling over the edge, waves of pleasure radiating through my body.

We lie in a tangle of limbs, chests heaving. My heart swells with love for this complicated, dangerous man. No matter our difficulties, we will always find our way back to each other.

Jack kisses my forehead, smoothing my hair away from my face. "Get some rest," he says. "You'll need it for tomorrow."

My eyes flutter closed, and I drift off to sleep in Jack's arms. The troubles of the day fade into the darkness, overpowered by the peace of this moment. Unfortunately, it doesn't last.

25

Emily

My pulse quickens with each step as I make my way up the winding path to Sarah's house, a prickle of unease dancing across my skin. I've known Sarah since kindergarten. Certainly, if she suspected I'd slept with Will, she wouldn't have agreed to see me. She would have made an excuse, brushed me off. But she didn't. Nevertheless, the weight of my secrets bears down upon my shoulders, their whispered accusations echoing in my mind.

I shift the tray of food in my hands, my knuckles whitening around its edges. The casserole dish emits a tantalizing aroma, but I find no comfort in its scent. All I taste is the bitterness of regret. *What was I thinking? What kind of person sleeps with their best friend's husband?*

Sarah opens the door before I have a chance to knock, her eyes rimmed red from crying. She glances at the dish in my hand.

"Emily, you shouldn't have." Her smile falters for a moment, a flicker of sorrow etching lines around her mouth.

I swallow against the lump forming in my throat. "I wanted to make sure you and Ian were taken care of." The lie slips easily from my lips, though its bitter aftertaste does little to assuage my guilt.

Sarah steps aside to let me in, her hand resting briefly on my arm. "You're the best, Em."

I stiffen at her touch, her words piercing my armor of deception. My fingers tighten around the tray as I struggle to maintain my composure.

Sarah guides me toward the kitchen, oblivious to my inner turmoil. "Ian's sleeping, so I'll make us some tea."

She takes the casserole from my hands, concern furrowing her brow. "You look pale. Are you feeling all right?"

I force a smile, though it does little to mask the uneasiness lurking beneath. "I'm okay. Just worried about you."

Sarah busies herself preparing tea, her back to me. I watch her every movement, alert for any signs of suspicion. But she shows no indication of feeling anything other than being happy I'm here. What a relief.

She turns and presses a cup into my hands. "Here. Chamomile tea. It will help you relax."

I nod gratefully, wrapping my fingers around the warmth seeping into my palms. The heat soothes my frayed edges, steadying my resolve.

I follow Sarah into the living room and settle onto the sofa beside her. "I'm glad you came," she says, crossing and uncrossing her legs.

"Of course. That's what friends are for."

"Mom had to drive Dad to physical therapy. It feels weird to be alone, but I couldn't take another second of Will's dad being here, so I sent him home."

I set my mug on the coffee table, brushing my palms across my knees. "Rachel told me Will's father has some interesting theories."

"And so do I," she says. "But I don't really want to talk about that. I could really use a distraction from it all, to be honest."

"Yeah, I get it…"

"I really don't know what I would do without you—or Rach." Her eyes glisten with tears as she speaks, sorrow etched into the lines of her face. "Ava, on the other hand…"

Guilt rises like bile in my throat. I swallow hard against the acrid taste, forcing it back down into the dark recesses of my soul. "She means well."

"I know. But she thinks Brian dying is the same as Will being brutally murdered and it's not, Em. It's just not."

"I'm so sorry for your loss." The words ring hollow, a meaningless platitude in the face of grief I helped inflict. But I don't know what else to say besides the obvious. "Will was a good man. He didn't deserve this."

Sarah shakes her head, blinking back tears. "No, he didn't. But dwelling on how undeserved his death is will not bring him back."

She takes a shaky breath, her composure wavering. "All we can do now is find out what happened and make sure his killer pays for what they've done."

A chill seeps into my bones at her words. She cannot know the role I played in Will's demise, if, in fact, Jack is at fault. I watch her closely, searching for any sign that she suspects my involvement.

"The police will find who did this," I say, taking her hand in mine. I give it a gentle squeeze. "We have to believe that."

She looks at me with gratitude and something else I can't quite decipher. "Can you stay awhile? My parents should be back soon…"

"Of course. I can stay as long as you need me to."

Sarah's gaze drifts to the baby monitor on the table beside her.

For a moment, a shadow crosses her features. Then she looks at me again, eyes shining with warmth that cuts like a knife.

"Ian is the one good thing I have left." Her voice trembles slightly. "I don't know how I would go on without him."

Guilt coils in my stomach at the mention of her child, a reminder of the future that has been taken from the both of them. I cling to my purpose, a lifeline in the sea of doubts threatening to engulf me. I am here to be a friend. I remind Sarah that justice will be served—that whoever murdered Will must pay for their crimes. But the truth is, I wonder whether it even matters. The damage is done.

"You're strong," I say. "You'll get through this, for Ian's sake and your own."

She nods, blinking away tears. Silence falls between us, weighted with unspoken truths until finally Sarah exhales a long breath. "What happened Friday night, Em? I'd had a lot to drink, and possibly I did a few things I regret, but you were with Will... Did he say anything—act odd—anything? How was he?"

"He—"

The baby monitor crackles to life, Ian's cries drifting into the room. Sarah rises swiftly, the lines of grief and worry easing from her features. She waits for me to speak, but Ian's wailing only grows louder. Eventually, she glances toward his room. "I should get him."

I nod, watching as she disappears down the hall, leaving me alone with the ruins of our friendship. As I sit waiting for her to return, I realize Sarah asked how Will was—*not* whether I slept with him. I sense she suspects something happened, but also that she doesn't really want to know, and I realize that maybe I'm doing her a small kindness by concealing the truth.

I came here prepared to confess what I'd done if it came to that.

Now, I see things differently. Will is dead, which is terrible enough. Why make things worse for her? What good will it do?

Regardless, the conversation is destined to continue, and I can't help but think the universe did me a favor with the baby waking when he did.

26

Emily

I glance at the family photo of Sarah, Will, and baby Ian on the end table, and I can't help but smile. I'd snapped the picture at a dinner party at Rachel's four months ago, had it framed, and presented it to Sarah for Mother's Day.

She cried when she opened it.

I lift it from the table, studying the smirk on Will's face, the happiness in Sarah's eyes. That was back when things were good. Or so I thought. Will and Jack had just started working together on a project. Will was putting in most of the sweat equity while Jack was funding the venture.

Jack had been happy with the deal, excited about the project, pleased to have something to fill his time. Until he wasn't.

"Will has been exorbitant in his requests," Jack complained. "He thinks he deserves more money than he does. He's pissing off the contractors, and when I brought it up, he offered to buy me out.

But I'd hardly call it an offer. It's pathetic, and quite frankly, insulting."

"I don't think he's trying to cheat you," I said. "He just wants to make sure his family is taken care of. That's all."

Jack scoffed. "There are other ways of taking care of your family."

I sighed. "Will has a family to support, Jack. We don't need the money, why make this so difficult?"

"That's not the point."

While I didn't agree entirely, I respected where my husband was coming from. Or at least I tried. Sarah, being a childhood friend, was far more important to me than that sum of money. So, I tried to assure Jack that Will's offer was reasonable. Unfortunately, Jack has always been more a man of principle than reason.

So I offered him a compromise, one he couldn't refuse, if he agreed to accept the offer and walk away without rocking the boat.

Rachel was hosting one of her famous dinner parties, and I promised Jack something in return if he would just go and enjoy himself, and, most importantly, if there was no talk of business.

"What are you offering me, exactly?" Jack had a mischievous twinkle in his eye. "Another night at the opera?"

I smiled as I shook my head. "Why don't you come over here and find out for yourself," I replied coyly.

Looking at the photo, I can see it was a good call. The evening was full of laughter and fun, so much so that it was almost like old times. It also helped that I was certain I was pregnant. All night, I refused drinks when offered.

The memory catches me by surprise, and the walls of Sarah's living room start to close in around me. Shadows dance at the edges of my vision. I grip the armrests of the sofa, struggling for breath. The air feels heavy and oppressive, dense with secrets that threaten to suffocate me, until it feels like I have to get out of here.

I promised Sarah I would stay.

I rise on unsteady feet and make my way to the kitchen, where I busy myself with emptying our mugs of tea, even though both have gone mostly untouched. I know it will look suspicious if I were to bolt now, so I temper from the urge to run by tidying up the kitchen.

Soon, Sarah comes in, Ian nestled against her chest.

"You didn't have to do that," she says, gesturing toward the dishes.

"It's the least I could do."

The phone rings, startling us both. Sarah fishes her cell from the kitchen table, shuffling Ian in her arms. She looks at the phone and then at me. "Would you mind?" she says, sliding the baby my way. "I need to take this."

"Are you kidding?" I reposition Ian in my arms, leaning down to inhale his sweet scent as I do. "There's nothing I'd rather do."

When Sarah leaves, the baby fusses, so I make a bottle, one-handed, which I've seen Sarah do a thousand times. I'm struck by how easy she's always made it look.

As I sit feeding him, a memory plays on a loop in my mind, each detail etched into my consciousness. I can still see the glint of the knife as it sliced through flesh and bone. The metallic scent of blood fills my senses, as vivid as if I were standing in that alleyway again.

A sharp intake of breath, the desperation in those eyes staring into mine, pleading for mercy. The feeble grasp of fingers clenching at my sleeve, a last futile attempt to cling to life.

And then silence. Stillness where there was once a beating heart.

I killed a man. Extinguished a life before its time. It wasn't the first time, nor would it be the last.

I try to shake the memory, but it clings to me like a second skin. The boundaries between now and then blur, the past and present folding into each other. I'm back in that alley, the weight of what I've done pressing down upon my shoulders.

I can still see the knife as it slips from my fingers, clattering to the ground. But the blood remains, a silent accusation that stains my hands. No matter how hard I scrub, the crimson hue will not fade.

It wasn't supposed to be my kill, and still, to this day, although Jack swears he got food poisoning from my friend's cooking, I can't help but feel like he set me up that night, that it was just another of his many tests.

Just hours before, I had been talking and pacing around our living room with Jack for what seemed like days, but had only been a few minutes. We were discussing the plan that I had come up with—always Jack's favorite topic of discussion, delivering justice as murder—and the best way to go about it.

Earlier that week, while we were stopped at an intersection, a panhandler had swung an ax at our car. Jack was certain that the man was dangerous and had to be dealt with, while I was certain that he was mentally ill and should get help instead. Jack argued that they no longer put such people in institutions, and I countered that we could have the man arrested and locked away if he was truly a danger.

"He'll just be out the next day, swinging the ax at the next car," Jack said. "And we'll be funding it all—rinse, lather, repeat."

The discussion continued on until we both finally agreed that if Jack would go to Rachel's dinner party, and if he could stay out of any conversations about business, then I would come up with the plan for murdering the panhandler. Jack would carry it out.

It seemed like a fair compromise to both of us, but I was hesitant, torn between wanting to make Jack happy and feeling that what we were about to do was wrong. My heart just wasn't in it. Not for any particular reason, but more like when someone suggests Italian food for dinner, but you're in the mood for Chinese.

In the end, I relented, and we drafted a rough plan of our attack while debating the morality of what we were about to do.

Jack was sure that this was the only way for him to feel safe about me passing that intersection every day, and he wanted justice to be served.

We ended up returning to the intersection, but this time, instead of an ax, the man had an actual sword. "So, he's arming himself," I said. "It's not illegal."

But just as soon as the words left my lips, the man pointed his sword at the truck in front of us and punctured the tires.

Needless to say, Jack won.

I tried to distract myself with thoughts of the dinner party, but my mind kept returning to the task ahead. I could not help but feel a sense of dread as I realized that in a number of hours, Jack and I would be standing in the shadows, waiting to stab a man to death.

Jack and I had gone over the plan one final time before we hit the streets. "Are you ready?" he asked, his voice composed but firm.

"As ready as I'm ever going to be," I replied with a nervous chuckle, feeling my insides knot up despite my attempt at humor.

We silently gathered our supplies— gloves, a knife, a change of clothing—all the items necessary for what was about to take place. At one point, I offered to go to the dinner party alone, but Jack refused. His silence spoke volumes; he knew that if he weren't there keeping a watchful eye on me, I might just back out of our agreement.

By the time night had fallen, I was ready to do whatever it took to get through it. Jack and I had reviewed the details of the plan one last time before getting ready to leave. I was ambivalent, but I was determined to get it over with. I knew that my life, and Jack's, would never be the same. I was convinced I was pregnant and this would be the last kill for Jack and I. But I couldn't have been more wrong.

27

Emily

Sarah returns to the kitchen, looking at me through red-rimmed eyes. Mascara stains streak down her cheeks, a visible reminder of her anguish.

"The coroner called." Her voice breaks on a sob, and she sinks into a chair. "They are releasing Will's body. He said it's ready for burial."

The finality of her words hit me like a blow. I take a seat beside her, grasping for words that won't come.

"I'm so sorry, Sarah." The apology rings hollow, a meaningless platitude in the face of such irrevocable loss. "If there's anything I can do..."

"Just stay with me." She reaches for my hand, clinging to it like a lifeline. "I don't want to be alone. Losing Will…it's like losing a part of myself."

Her grief pierces my heart, sharpened by the knowledge of my complicity. I gave Will what he wanted, surrendering to passion with reckless abandon. If only I'd refused his advances, stayed true to Jack, I don't think any of this would have happened.

The memory of that night haunts me, the warmth of Will's embrace, the hunger in his kiss, the soft whisper of promises we had no right to make. We were meant to be together, he said.

No one makes me feel the way you do.

Lies. All of it lies and empty promises.

"He loved you so much." I swallow against the tightness in my throat, choking back tears I have no right to shed. "You were his whole world."

"Then why?" She clutches at me, her nails biting into my skin. "Why did he have to die? Who could hate him that much?"

I turn away, unable to meet her gaze. "I don't know. But the police will find Will's killer and he will pay for what he's done."

Will's killer. The words mock me, an accusation I cannot escape. I may not have murdered him, but I am not the person Sarah thinks I am. It's only a matter of time until she sees the truth, realizing the monster she's embraced as a friend.

"My life will never be the same," she chokes out between sobs.

"No," I say. "It won't. But things won't always be this bad."

"How can you know that?"

I don't know how to answer. I've woven a tangled web of lies, ensnaring us all, and I feel there's no escape.

The darkness has already won.

So, once again, I lie. "I just do."

28

Anonymous

Admittedly, she looks very unwell. I watch as she exits the house, the weight of guilt threatening to crush her. Each step is a battle, her limbs leaden beneath its relentless press.

In the solitude of her car, the mask falls away. Tears gather and spill, dripping onto her leather seats in a silent cascade. The sobs rack her body, a futile attempt to purge the poison from her veins.

But it is too late. The rot has already set in, devouring her from the inside out.

I know what she's thinking. I can see the darkness closing in, whispering of endings and release. Perhaps it would be better to go to the police, to tell them what she knows.

No more ghosts. No more secrets. No more blood on her hands.

The thought is tempting, a siren's call luring her toward the rocks. She grips the steering wheel like an anchor holding her in place.

Then I notice it—the slight shake of her head followed by a swipe of her hand on her face and the swift straightening of her spine. She won't give in—not yet.

She starts the car, peeling away from the curb. In the rearview mirror, the house recedes into the distance, a grim monument to choices that can never be undone.

She doesn't realize she's being followed. At least not at first.

I will follow her to the ends of the earth, if that's what it takes.

I know what she's capable of. I've seen the darkness inside her. And I can't let her go unchecked.

I follow her through the winding roads of the city, keeping a safe distance. Her car is a blur of red in front of me, and I can see her head occasionally bobbing to the beat of the music. It's a strange contrast to the turmoil I know is inside her.

As we approach a parking lot, her car suddenly swerves into it. I park a few spots away, watching as she exits the car and walks toward a nondescript building. I can see her hand shaking as she fumbles with the lock, eventually pushing the door open and disappearing inside.

I wait for a few minutes before following her. The hallway is empty, but I can hear muffled voices coming from one of the doors. I make my way toward the source of the noise, my heart pounding in my chest.

I press my ear against the door, trying to make out what they're saying. It's a man and a woman, their voices low and urgent. I can hear crying, and I know by the sound it's her.

"I can't do this anymore," she sobs. "I can't keep living like this."

"We don't have a choice," he replies. "We have to keep going until it's done."

Panic rises in her voice as she speaks. "What if we get caught?"

"We won't," he says firmly. "We've been doing this for years. We know how to cover our tracks."

29

Emily

The incessant ticking of the clock on our living room wall feels like needles piercing my eardrums. Days pass. It has been nearly a week since we found Will dead.

Jack is at the office, leaving me alone with my thoughts and the oppressive silence that suffocates me. I can't escape the feeling of being watched, as if someone is peering through the windows, scrutinizing my every move.

Shame and guilt weigh heavily on my mind, like a leaden fog. Remembering the feeling of Will's hands on my body, knowing how deeply and completely I betrayed Sarah, my oldest and dearest friend, fills me with a self-loathing that is indescribable.

An icy dread settles in my stomach like a heavy stone when I think about being unfaithful to Jack. Will's death feels like a punishment for my transgressions, which is only compounded by my knowledge that I'll never be able to have a family with the man I love if I stay. Although I want freedom from the darkness of our past, part of me fears that Jack will never allow it—we are fundamentally too similar, bound together by shared secrets and crimes. He will never let me go. A split between us would not be as simple as a divorce or an exit tax. I would likely pay with my life.

But even if I stay, it is only a matter of time before everything implodes—before it all blows up in my face. There seems to be no way out, no escape from the mounting evidence leading the police straight to us. I am trapped.

It's only half past ten, but I clutch a tumbler of whiskey, the amber liquid sloshing against the ice cubes. The fiery burn of alcohol scalds my throat, but it does little to numb my frayed nerves. I couldn't sleep last night. I haven't slept in almost a week. I can't concentrate. Images of Will's lifeless body haunt me, plaguing me with guilt that clings to me like a second skin.

I've never been much of a drinker, but I need something to settle my nerves, so I down the rest of the whiskey. It's not much, just enough to dull the edges. The glass clinks against the coffee table as I set it down with trembling hands. I have to be at work by one. It's only my second day back at the office, and I cannot call in again. Not if I want to keep my job.

I head upstairs to get ready, calling Jack on the way up. He answers on the first ring. We're both a little jumpy lately. "Jack, I think we're being watched," I whisper. He dismisses my concerns with a sigh, telling me I'm just stressed and need to relax.

"Emily, you're letting your imagination get the better of you," he says, his voice distant.

But I don't think so.

Nonetheless, I get ready and head to the office.

When my assistant tells me Detective Alvarez is waiting for me in the conference room, my heart skips a beat, and I almost think she's mistaken.

I step into the room, closing the door behind me with a soft click that seems to echo through every corner of my being. The predatory gleam in his eyes is enough to make my skin crawl.

"Mrs. Brown, I hope I haven't interrupted anything important," Alvarez says, and I can't help noticing how his words are as cold and sharp as a blade. My throat goes dry, and I swallow hard, forcing a smile that feels more like a grimace. "But I had a few questions..."

"Right. Sure. Of course." I take the seat across from him, trying to maintain an air of calm, but my hands tremble as I reach for a pen, attempting to appear busy. I assume that he hasn't spoken with Jack, and I know why. Alvarez senses weakness in me that he doesn't see in my husband. He's come for the low hanging fruit.

"We've been making progress on Will's murder case, and I wanted to make sure I have everything straight."

My breath catches in my throat, and I force myself to nod, gripping the pen so tightly ink spills out. "Yeah. Whatever you need."

He produces a printout, which I recognize immediately. It's a copy of the rental's floor plan. "Can you point out which of the bedrooms you and Mr. Brown occupied during your stay?" The question is blunt, and his gaze never wavers from mine, searching for any sign of deceit.

"It was this one here," I say, which is the truth, but the way Alvarez's eyes narrow makes it feel like a lie.

"Interesting. Did you have any conversations with Will prior to the eighteenth? Any text messages or calls?"

I shrug then shake my head, feeling the weight of his suspicion like a noose around my neck. "Um...well, we were friends—I mean, we spoke occasionally. Mostly through group chats."

"Very well. I'll be in touch if we have more questions." Alvarez pushes away from the table and turns to leave, pausing at the door to cast one last searching glance in my direction. "You know, I really am sorry about your loss. I hated to bother you at work."

The door closes behind him, and I'm left with the suffocating silence of my thoughts. My mind races through a thousand desperate scenarios, each one more horrifying than the last as the image of prison bars closing in around me becomes an all-consuming fear.

In the days that follow, the crushing weight of impending imprisonment sends my once-thriving career into a downward spiral. During important meetings, my formerly confident voice is reduced to a trembling whisper, drowned out by the whispers of suspicion from those around me.

Concentration becomes an elusive beast, and I find myself staring at my computer screen for hours on end, typing and deleting fragmented ideas and irrational fears.

"Emily, are you okay?" The concern etched on my assistant's face only heightens my paranoia, and I brush off her inquiry with a strained smile.

"I'm fine. Just...a lot on my mind." It's a lie, but the truth is a luxury I can no longer afford.

30

Emily

I sink into my chair and drop my head into my hands, massaging my temples. The headache pounding behind my eyes is reaching new heights, fueled by stress and lack of sleep.

When was the last time I ate a decent meal? Showered? The days are blurring together, time slipping through my fingers as fast as the deals I can no longer hold on to.

My phone rings, startling me from my thoughts. I snatch up the receiver, pulse skipping. "Hello?"

"Emily, it's Mark. We need to talk about the Ellerman deal. The clients are getting impatient, and if we don't have a term sheet in front of them by the end of the week, they're taking it to another firm. I thought you were on top of this..."

His tone is equal parts concern and irritation. I swallow hard, scrambling for a response. Everything is falling apart. "I'm so sorry, Mark, you're right. I've had...a personal issue I've been dealing with, but I'm back on track now. I'll have the terms to you within two days, I promise."

Silence. Then, "I hope everything's all right. But we're all under a lot of pressure here, Emily. We're counting on you. Please don't let us down."

The line goes dead. I stare at the phone in my hand, Mark's words echoing in my mind.

Don't let us down.

Too late. I'm already drowning, the currents of my chaotic mind pulling me under as I struggle to keep my head above water. But the truth is, I stopped treading water a long time ago.

Now I'm just sinking.

My phone rings again. It's my assistant, letting me know I was supposed to be in a meeting with our CFO fifteen minutes ago. Everyone is waiting in the conference room, wondering where I am.

The fluorescent lights in the boardroom buzz loudly, as piercing as a dentist's drill. Sweat trickles down my neck and soaks into the collar of my blouse as I take my seat.

"Emily," Mr. Chen says. "We're so glad you could finally join us."

Michael Chen, my boss, has this thing about what he calls B players. You do not want to be one, and right now that's exactly how he's looking at me. Never mind that I've given this company nearly a decade of my life. There is no room for error. No time to step off the ladder.

My gaze darts around the room, searching for escape. But there are too many eyes on me, judging me, their whispers like a swarm of mosquitoes buzzing in my ear.

I swallow and clench my trembling hands under the table. I listen as my colleagues drone on about quarterly earnings and new client acquisitions, but their voices fade into the background.

All I can hear is the pounding of my heart, a primal drumbeat urging me to run. But I'm trapped.

Mr. Chen peers at me over the rim of his glasses, bushy eyebrows raised in expectation. I stare back at him, my mind blank. What did he ask me?

The room tilts and spins. I grip the edge of the table, my nails screaming in protest.

My boss's frown deepens. "Mrs. Brown, are you all right? You look rather pale."

I force a stiff smile and nod. "Of course, my apologies. What was the question?"

But the words swim before my eyes, incomprehensible. A metallic taste fills my mouth as nausea rises in my throat.

The walls close in around me, the fluorescent lights blinding me, the whispers deafening. I push back from the table and mumble an excuse, bolting from my seat.

Mr. Chen calls after me, his voice laced with concern, but I don't stop.

I race down the hallway, heels clicking sharply against the marble floor, echoing in the empty corridor like a countdown to my demise.

At last, the restroom. I burst through the door and brace myself against the counter, gasping for breath.

The walls won't stop closing in. It feels like I'm going to die in here, trapped in this gleaming mausoleum of corporate ambition.

A stall creaks behind me. I freeze in place, my heart pounding so loudly it threatens to drown out all the other sounds.

I'm not alone.

I force myself to turn around, slowly, so slowly my joints scream in protest.

A figure looms in the stall, silhouetted in shadows. I blink hard, trying to clear my vision, but the silhouette remains.

My voice emerges as a trembling whisper. "Who's there?"

No response. The figure stands motionless, watching and waiting.

I take a step forward. Close and open my eyes again.

The restroom is empty.

I lean against the counter, drawing deep breaths to slow my racing heart. It was only my imagination, fueled by paranoia and sleep deprivation. Jack is right. The stress is getting to me.

But was it my imagination?

The stall creaks behind me again. I whip around, peering in.

Nothing.

My pulse thrums in my ears as I scrutinize the room. All clear.

I turn to face the mirror, wiping cold sweat from my brow. My reflection stares back at me, pale and hollow-eyed, a stranger in familiar skin.

Another creak shatters the silence. I stare at my reflection in the mirror, wide-eyed, frozen in place.

There, in the mirror's reflection, a shadowy figure looms behind me, face obscured by a dark hood.

I squeeze my eyes shut, willing the apparition away. When I open them again, the reflection shows only my pale, frightened face staring back at me. *What have I become?* I make a mental note to search for signs of a mental breakdown when I return to my computer. For now, I splash cold water on my face, taking deep breaths to steady my frayed nerves. The walls seem to close in around me as tremors rack my body. I need to get out of here. Now.

As I reach for the door handle, I hear movement behind me. I freeze in place, pulse pounding, afraid to turn around.

Silence.

Then, a rustle of fabric and the scrape of a shoe against marble.

Getting closer.

I lunge for the door and yank it open, stumbling into the hallway. When I look back, the restroom is empty. Light spills from the open door to reveal bare walls and tile.

There's no one there.

Laughter rises in my throat, bordering on hysteria. I really am losing my mind.

How am I supposed to function like this?

As I head back to my office, the whispers start, harsh voices riding on the heels of my footsteps.

Murderer.

Liar.

You'll never escape what you've done.

I quicken my pace, nearly breaking into a jog. The voices chase me down the hallway, gaining momentum. My heart pounds as I burst through the door of my office and slam it behind me, the whispers fading into silence.

Chest heaving, I lean against the door and squeeze my eyes shut. No more. I can't take any more of this.

There's only one way to silence the voices and put an end to this all.

I have to find Will's actual killer.

31

Jack

The somber atmosphere of Will's memorial service engulfs us as Emily and I cross the threshold into the church. It almost feels wrong to be here. Grief hangs heavy in the air like a shroud, smothering every breath as we pay our respects. Staring at my trembling wife, concern for her mental state gnaws at me, yet suspicion creeps in like an unwelcome shadow.

Did she really murder Will? And if so, why won't she just admit it?

The thoughts awaken a dark fascination within me, fueling my desire to uncover the truth.

Ava, Lucas, Rachel, and Sarah—Emily's friends—huddle together, their faces etched with grief. Tension crackles between Ava and Sarah, their gazes icy and fraught with animosity. I watch with keen interest as Lucas and Rachel engage in strained conversation, masking their true feelings beneath forced smiles. My contempt for them intensifies, finding validation in the fractures within their relationships.

Eventually, *finally*, the service begins. The minister drones on, spewing generic platitudes about Will's untimely death. I can feel the weight of my eyes fixated on Emily, dissecting her every move, searching for signs of guilt or deception. She sits stoically, her eyes glistening with unshed tears. Her vulnerability peeks out from time to time, and I find myself captivated by the darkness lurking within her.

"Emily," I say, reaching out to touch her arm.

She flinches at my touch, averting her gaze and wiping away a stray tear. "Yeah?"

"Are you all right?" I ask, feigning concern while my heart races in anticipation of what might be revealed.

"Of course," she says, her voice cracking under the strain. "I'm just...it's all so...overwhelming."

I nod, letting Emily believe she has successfully concealed her emotions.

As the service continues, the minister eventually shuts up and we move to the congregation hall for refreshments. I detach myself from the somber atmosphere, shifting my focus to the unraveling dynamics between Emily and her friends.

"It's such a tragedy," Ava says, dabbing at her eyes with a delicate handkerchief as I approach her. "Reminds me of Brian's funeral."

"Absolutely." I study her. "I imagine the occasion is especially difficult for Sarah. But here you are, making it all about you."

Ava stiffens, her icy gaze locking onto mine. "Excuse me?"

"Nothing," I say, waving a dismissive hand. "Just making an observation."

"Please, keep your observations to yourself," she snaps before walking away.

Moments later, Rachel wanders over. "Jack, have you seen Emily?" she asks, her eyes darting around the room.

"Last I checked, she was speaking with the minister," I respond nonchalantly. "Why? Is something wrong?"

"Nothing, just wanted to check on her." She folds her arms over her chest. "She's been ignoring my calls."

"Em's just been busy with work. I wouldn't take it personally." Her eyes flitter back to me. "Right."

I watch Emily across the room, her hands wringing the fabric of her black dress, and an image flashes in my mind. I know my wife; I've known her for a long time. I don't need an outright confession. As the saying goes: A guilty conscience needs no accuser. She must pay for her betrayal, for sleeping with Will. The same as Rachel must pay for drugging me. Or at least for being aware it was going to happen. *How* is the question. What kind of retribution is sufficient for that kind of evil? The possibilities dance like shadows in my mind, each darker than the last.

"Jack?" A voice breaks through my thoughts, pulling me back to reality. It's Michael, our chef—or rather, our former chef. He hasn't been back to work since he found Will's body. His eyes are rimmed red, but there's an undeniable fire in them. "Could I have a word with you?"

"Ah, Michael," I say with a tight smile. "What can I do for you?"

"Look, man, I want my job back." He glares at me with an intensity that would be almost comical if it weren't so misplaced. "This whole thing has been a nightmare, but I've got bills to pay. I *need* this job."

"Your job?" I chuckle darkly. "In the grand scheme of things, that seems rather trivial, doesn't it?"

"Trivial?" he scoffs. "It's my livelihood!"

"I'm aware," I say, taking pleasure in his agitation. Truth is, I never liked the guy, and I didn't think his food was all that great. Emily, on the other hand… "Well, I'll have to think about it."

"Think about it? " He repeats incredulously, his voice rising with anger. "I didn't kill anyone—I just found the body!"

"That's right," I say, my voice dripping with sarcasm. "An unfortunate coincidence, I'm sure." My mind briefly flirts with the idea of murdering Michael on the spot—after all, I've killed for far less. But we're already celebrating one dead guy. This hardly seems like the right venue.

"Please," he begs, desperation creeping into his voice. "I need this."

"I'll take your request under serious consideration."

Michael's face falls, his eyes darkening like storm clouds as he realizes the true weight of my words. "I know what happened that night," he quips. "I know what you guys were up to—the swinging..."

"Swinging?"

"Yeah, sleeping with other people."

"You must be mistaken."

"But you see, I'm not. I know y'all are keeping it from the cops, and it just seems like something they might want to know…"

"Tell you what—come by the house tomorrow evening and we'll see about your job, okay?"

He gives me a onceover, then nods stiffly and walks away.

As I watch him go, I can't help but feel a twisted sense of satisfaction. The shadows within me are stirring to life, and I can no longer deny my hunger for answers—or revenge—or the darkness that drives me forward. Michael should have known better than to threaten me. It hadn't turned out so well for the last guy.

32

Emily

Another week has come and gone. I stare into the depths of my coffee cup, the black liquid swirling like a vortex, threatening to engulf me. The incessant chatter at the café only serves to highlight my isolation, making me feel like a lone astronaut drifting further into the cold abyss of space. I'm supposed to be at work, but I'm so close to losing my job, I figured why bother? It's harder for them to fire you if you don't show up to hear the news.

I sip my coffee, wincing at the bitterness as it creeps down my throat, mirroring the darkness that continues to consume me from within.

"God, this tastes awful." I push away the cup in disgust. "I guess they're trying to match the ambiance of my life," I say to the woman at the table across from mine.

She gives me an odd look, reminding me that small talk among strangers is a thing of the past. Nowadays, it just makes you strange.

"I'm only here because my husband thinks I'm at the office, and I don't want to go home and give up the lie."

The woman shakes her head. "This isn't confession, lady, and I'm sure as hell not a priest."

I blink several times, trying to come up with a clever clap back. Once upon a time, it would have come naturally.

"Emily?" a familiar voice calls out. I look up to see Rachel approaching my table, her eyes wide with concern. "Is everything okay?"

"Absolutely peachy," I say with a forced smile. "Just mourning the loss of decent coffee in this godforsaken place."

Rachel shifts uncomfortably from foot to foot, unsure how to respond. It is evident that my once-charming sarcasm has turned caustic, isolating me further from those who care about me. Over the past few weeks, slowly, and then all at once, Ava, Sarah, and even Rachel have stopped taking my calls or responding to my texts.

"Listen, Em," she says, her voice wavering slightly. "I know you're having a hard time...but we're all worried about you. Wait"—she leans closer and scrunches her nose—"have you been drinking?"

"I don't know what you're talking about."

"Em—" I don't miss the hint of forced sympathy in her voice. "This is hard for everyone, but we can't let it destroy us."

"Destroy us?" I scoff, feeling my heart race. "How delightfully melodramatic. But don't worry, I'm just having a momentary lapse of sanity. All part of the grieving process, I'm sure."

I twist a strand of my long, dark hair around my finger, a nervous habit I'd developed since that weekend. "Besides, it's not what's destroying me. Someone's been following me..."

"So you've said."

"You think I'm crazy?"

"I don't know what to think."

"Yeah," I say, looking away. "Me neither."

"Look, we've been talking about getting together," Rachel says, dragging the chair across from me over the concrete floor. She sits down, trying to bridge the chasm that has formed. "You know, like old times. I think you should come, Em. It could help take your mind off things."

"Ah, yes," I say, my voice dripping with disdain. "A nostalgic trip down memory lane to when we were all blissfully ignorant of the cracks lurking beneath our perfect little lives. How quaint."

"Emily, please..." Rachel pleads, tears welling in her eyes. "I hate to see you like this."

"I think we should start telling the truth, Rach. Let the chips fall where they may."

This is exhibit A. The reason no one is taking my calls.

"I know you want to tell that detective the truth, but think of Sarah. Think of the embarrassment she'll face."

"Why should you care? She slept with your husband."

Rachel looks like I've backhanded her across the face. Exhibit B, why I've been an outcast. "And you slept with hers."

This makes me laugh. "I never claimed to be a saint."

The woman, who is *definitely* not a priest, studies me with a shrewd stare.

"So Sarah knows..."

Rachel nods. "I'd say she suspects."

Exhibit C why my calls are going unanswered. "I've tried reaching out to her," I say. "I've offered to watch the baby, to help with meals, whatever she needs, and…nothing. I get no response."

"The drinking doesn't help, Em. She says you're reminding her of Ava."

"Fine. But in that case—why won't Ava speak to me?"

She waves me off. "I don't know. Who knows with her." Rachel glances toward the door and then back at me. "Jack really offended her at Will's memorial service."

Shocker. "What's that got to do with me?"

"Are you kidding? You two are joined at the hip."

"I wouldn't exactly say that."

"Either way, I think we all need to talk—like Lucas said—before anyone talks to the cops again. We need to come up with a plan."

"Fine," I snap. "But if you think a get-together will magically fix everything, you're more delusional than I am."

"Thank you," Rachel whispers, relief washing over her face. "I'll text Ava and Sarah and set something up."

As I watch her walk away, I can't shake the insidious tendrils of doubt that have wormed their way into my consciousness. The feeling of being watched is ever-present, like an itch I can't quite scratch. My reflection in the café window seems to mock me, a twisted caricature of the woman I'd once been.

I try to ignore the gnawing sense of dread that has taken up residence in my chest. *Get a grip, Emily. Like Jack says, it's just your imagination running wild. No one's watching you.*

But as I catch sight of a shadowy figure lingering outside the café, a chill pricks my skin, making me question whether the gnawing feeling in my gut is truly unfounded. As the figure vanishes from view, I am left doubting my own sanity and wondering who—or what—is lurking just beyond my perception, waiting for the moment to strike.

"Paranoia is a cruel mistress," I say to the woman, struggling to maintain my composure. "And she isn't done with me yet."

It isn't long after that a man with kind eyes comes over and introduces himself as the manager. He apologizes, but tells me I am making the customers uncomfortable. I don't even recall what I say in response. But I do remember the look on the woman's face as I am politely escorted from the café.

33

Jack

I step through the front door of our home, the familiar scent of Emily's perfume mingling with the aroma of fresh-baked chocolate chip cookies wafting through the foyer.

The tension in my shoulders eases for a moment, a flicker of nostalgia transporting me to happier times. But the illusion shatters as the whispers begin anew, the walls seeming to breathe secrets between us. The mask of normalcy Emily clings to is slipping further with each passing day.

Her eyes dart nervously to meet mine, her fingers twisting the diamond band on her left hand. "How was your day, my love?" The endearment falls awkwardly from her lips, a relic from the past.

I shrug, scanning the foyer for any signs of disturbance. "Uneventful. Yours?"

"The same." Her smile doesn't reach her eyes. "I made your

favorite for dinner. Made-from-scratch chocolate chip cookies and lasagna."

My stomach churns at the thought of food. A familiar feeling stirs within, a reminder of what must be done to safeguard our fragile existence. "Did Michael stop by?"

"He was going to. But he sent a text saying something came up."

She lifts a cookie from the tray and holds it out.

"I'm not hungry."

Emily's face crumples. "I'm trying, Jack. I really am." Her voice cracks. "But I need you. The Jack I fell in love with. The Jack from before..."

"You mean *before* you slept with Will? Before you threatened to go to the police and tell them as much?"

Will's name has remained unspoken lately, a poison staining the space between us. My fingers clench at my sides, yearning to close around Emily's delicate throat. But I swallow the rage blistering my insides, and force a smile. "I'm here, Em. I've always been here."

The lie slips easily from my lips. But Emily's gaze sharpens, seeing beyond the facade. "That's not true."

"I met someone today," she says. "At the café. She'd be a good kill..."

I scoff as I am reminded of how good Emily has always been at getting what she wants. "Don't you think we're under enough scrutiny as it is?"

"No, Jack. I think another murder is exactly what the cops need. Spread their resources thin..."

"I don't think another distraction is what we need right now. You're barely holding it together as it is."

"You know what I think? I think you can never be happy. No matter what I say—or what I do—it's never enough!"

"Oh, believe me, you've done enough."

"Fuck you." She brushes past me toward the living room, her

back straight, hands balled into fists. "At least you can't say I didn't try!"

"Was fucking Will a part of your effort? Because if that's the case, sweetheart, you've done a bang-up job."

"Are we even going to talk about how you had a vasectomy and lied to me about it for *years*? Every month I wasn't pregnant, you let me think it was my fault—that something was wrong with *me!*"

"What's there to talk about? Why would I want to have a kid with someone I can't trust—someone low enough to screw *Will* of all people?"

Emily flips on her heel. She watches me for a second and then narrows her eyes. "It's too bad," she says, "that it couldn't have been you that died."

Her words slice like a razor. But I won't give her the satisfaction of a response. Instead, I watch as she pounds up the stairs to our bedroom and slams the door behind her. The walls seem to tilt and spin, whispers morphing into shrieks. My pulse thrums wildly, the darkness spreading through my veins like a cancer. In this moment, I know with stark certainty there is only one way to silence the issues threatening to consume us both. At some point, we all have to choose between love and self-preservation.

Emily is a liability. She must be dealt with as such.

34

Jack

I stand motionless in the foyer, Emily's parting words echoing in my mind. Our home—once a symbol of love and new beginnings—has transformed into a graveyard haunted by ghosts. The life we dreamed of building together lies in ruins, betrayed by secrets and suspicion. It's maddening, but predictable. Nothing good lasts forever.

By the time I've cleaned the kitchen and put away dinner, Emily still has herself holed up in our room.

The stairs creak under my feet as I climb toward our bedroom. Moonlight filters through the windows, casting shadows that seem to whisper and move. My heart pounds against my ribcage, a caged beast struggling to break free. I find the door unlocked, Emily sitting at the edge of our bed, her shoulders slumped in defeat.

She startles at the sound of my footsteps, peering up at me through a veil of tears. "Jack, I—I'm sorry. I didn't mean..." Her voice trails off as she searches my face, no doubt noticing the rigid set of my jaw or the cold detachment in my eyes.

I cross the room in three swift strides, grasping Emily's arm in a bruising grip. She cries out, confusion and fear chasing across her features. I give her arm a sharp twist, relishing the gasp of pain escaping her lips. "The time for apologies is over, Em." My voice emerges low and rough, barely recognizable. "You, of all people, should know there are things you can't take back. You are right. It is too bad."

"Yeah, well, some truths are universal and take a while to learn."

I can't help but laugh at the defiance in her eyes. "Do I look like I'm in a joking mood?"

Emily struggles in my grasp, her breaths coming in short, panicked bursts. "Jack, you're hurting me! What are you doing?"

"Was it the lasagna or the cookies you flavored with ricin? Or both?"

"What?" Fear flashes in her eyes, and behind it I spot the lie. "Neither! How can you accuse me of that?"

I shove her onto the bed, pinning her in place with my body. Emily's screams pierce the air, shrill and desperate. But we are alone here, the house veiled in silence. No one will come to her aid. No one will hear her last cries.

My fingers wrap around Emily's throat, squeezing with relentless pressure. She claws at my hands, writhing beneath me, but her strength is no match for my own. Darkness bleeds into the edges of my vision as Emily's face turns an alarming shade of blue. The whispers fade into blissful nothingness, leaving only the frantic beat of my heart.

Her hands fall limp at her sides, her eyes glassy and fixed. I release my grip, sitting back on my heels as I survey the ruin of the woman I once loved. And in the silence, there is peace.

I stand abruptly, shaken from the trance that had settled over my mind. *What have I done?*

BLOOD, SWEAT, AND DESIRE: A PSYCHOLOGICAL THRILLER

Emily's lifeless body lies splayed across our bed, pale and still against the dark sheets. The woman I vowed to cherish and protect, now broken beyond repair. Bile rises in my throat at the sight, a wave of horror and revulsion threatening to overwhelm me.

My hands tremble as I reach out to brush a strand of hair from her face, half expecting her eyes to flutter open. But she remains motionless, all traces of the vibrancy that once lit her from within extinguished by my hands. I stumble back from the bed, chest heaving with panicked breaths.

How did it come to this?

I scrub a hand over my face, willing myself to think. But my mind is blank, thoughts scattering like leaves in the wind. Emily is dead, and I am at fault. There can be no going back from this.

The walls seem to close in around me, the air thick with the metallic scent of blood. I have to get out of here. Now.

I rush from the room without looking back, grabbing my keys and wallet on the way out. My hands shake as I start the car, peeling out of the driveway and into the night. I don't know where I'm going, only that I need to escape. To forget the lifeless eyes that will haunt my dreams. To outrun the demons nipping at my heels.

The road stretches endlessly before me, a twisting snake of asphalt cutting through the darkness. I press the gas pedal to the floor. The speedometer climbs higher and higher, the world around me reduced to a blur.

But no matter how fast I drive, I cannot escape the truth. I've just killed the only woman I've ever loved. The only woman I'll *ever* love.

I drive without direction, lost in a maze of back roads as I try to outrun my thoughts. But there is no escape. Emily's lifeless eyes follow me, a silent accusation that echoes in my mind.

You did this.

I clench my jaw against the voice, hands trembling around the steering wheel. The needle on the speedometer climbs higher and higher, my foot pressing the gas pedal to the floor. The world blurs into a smear of colors as I hurtle down the road, trees and signs passing in a flash.

But no speed is fast enough. No distance significant enough. I cannot outrun those watchful eyes.

The road swims before me, tears blurring my vision. *Fuck.* I swipe at them angrily, cursing the weakness that threatens to overtake me. I squeeze my eyes shut for a moment, trying to block out the image of Emily's pale, lifeless face.

When I open my eyes again, I'm greeted with the sight of a hairpin turn barreling toward me. I jerk the steering wheel to the side, tires squealing in protest. The car begins to spin, slipping out of my control.

The world tilts and blurs, a kaleidoscope of shadows and light. There is the sharp scream of twisting metal, the air filled with the acrid scent of burning rubber.

Then everything goes black.

35

Jack

I come to with a start, disoriented and confused. My head pounds, a sharp pain piercing through the fog in my mind.

I blink my eyes open and find myself lying on the couch. It's still dark out.

Emily.

The memory crashes over me in a suffocating wave. I drag myself to my feet, stumbling as a surge of dizziness threatens to send me crashing to the floor.

"Emily?" My voice echoes through the house, hollow and desperate. No answer comes.

Dread pooling in my gut, I make my way upstairs. Our bedroom is empty, the bed neatly made as if waiting for occupants that will never arrive.

My heart lodges in my throat as I approach the guest bedroom. The door is slightly ajar, a sliver of light spilling from within.

Summoning every ounce of courage, I push the door open.

Emily lies on the bed, her limbs twisted in the silken sheets. Her eyes are closed, lips slightly parted, an expression of peace softening her features.

The walls begin to close in, the air turning stale and suffocating. As I watch the rise and fall of her chest, I stumble backward, exhaling a sigh of relief, trying to shake off the dream.

Numbness seeps into my bones as I stand in the doorway of our bedroom. Emily's scent lingers in the air, vanilla and jasmine with a hint of spice. I close my eyes, the nightmare flashing through my mind.

I try to focus on things that are real. Like Emily smiling up at me as we slow danced in our living room. Emily kissing me softly as snow fell around us on Christmas Eve. Emily's delighted laughter as I chased her through the poppy fields in Tuscany on our honeymoon.

I decide to let her sleep.

The staircase creaks under my feet as I descend into the foyer. Moonlight filters through the windows, casting shadows that lurk and slither. My fingers curl around the railing, fingers digging into the varnished surface.

As I reach the bottom step, a floorboard squeaks behind me. I whirl around to find Emily standing above me, pale and hollow-eyed in her silk robe.

My heart stutters. "Emily?"

She regards me with a detached calm. "Going somewhere?"

I clear my throat, pulse racing. "I couldn't sleep."

"Thanks to you, I couldn't either." She steps forward, and the light glints off the gun in her hand. My gut clenches in dread as she levels the barrel at my chest. "Thanks to you, I haven't slept in weeks."

I raise my hands in surrender, my mind scrambling. "Em, please. Put the gun down."

"Why?" Her finger curls around the trigger, rage simmering

beneath her placid veneer. "You were going to kill me, weren't you?"

The accusation sucker punches the air from my lungs. I stare at her, the woman I once knew consumed by madness and paranoia. There's no denying the truth. My silence is enough.

She aims the gun, lips twisting into a sneer. "You thought I wouldn't figure it out? All the clues you left, you may as well have signed your name." Her eyes blaze with fury. "Did you really think I'd make it easy for you?"

"No—"

She squeezes the trigger.

36

Emily

The cold metal of the gun presses against my palm, a manifestation of the consuming fear that has haunted me for weeks. My wide-eyed gaze fixates on it, heart pounding in my chest as I summon every ounce of courage to follow through with my intentions.

Jack raises his hands in surrender. "Em, please. Put the gun down."

"Why?" My finger curls around the trigger. "You were going to kill me, weren't you?"

He doesn't give me the dignity of an answer, which tells me everything I need to know.

"You thought I wouldn't figure it out? All the clues you left, you may as well have signed your name." My eyes blaze with fury. "Did you really think I'd make it easy for you?"

"No—"

"Emily," he says, his voice unnervingly calm despite the circumstances. "What are you doing?"

"Stay back!" I warn, clutching the gun tighter. "I just want to leave."

Jack's eyes narrow, the calculating wheels behind them turning. "You're not going anywhere, Emily. Not until we've talked about this."

He freezes in place, hands raised in surrender. But his eyes gleam with anger, lips curling into a snarl. "Put the gun down, Emily." His voice is deceptively calm, but laced with menace. "We both know you won't use it."

As Jack takes a step toward me, rage boils in my veins. "Stay away from me!" I shriek, leveling the gun at his chest.

The tense silence of our lavish home wraps around me like a suffocating fog. My trembling finger tightens around the trigger, but the hollow click reverberates through the air. *He's always thinking three steps ahead.*

Panic wells up inside me, a chilling dread taking hold, and my frantic eyes search for an escape. "Emily," he says, "you...you tried to kill me."

The air between us thickens, heavy with unspoken betrayal. My chest constricts, and I force myself to breathe. "You left me no choice. You're dangerous, Jack, and I can't live like this anymore!"

"Is that what you think?" he laughs. "That I'm a monster?"

"You emptied the gun."

"You avoided my question."

"Do I think you're a monster...hmmm...yes!" My words slice through the lingering silence. "All those people—"

"They weren't exactly pillars of the community, Emily," he interrupts, his tone defensive. "They were people who deserved it."

My heart pounds in my ears. "Who are you to decide that?"

"Someone had to do something!" He slams his fist against the wall. "I thought you understood that..."

"Maybe I did once," I whisper, my gaze falling to the cold marble floor. "But not anymore."

"What changed?" Jack demands, the hurt in his voice replaced by icy anger. "Was it me you stopped believing in or the cause?"

"Maybe I just realized what it was doing to us."

"Or maybe," he says, his voice dripping with venom, "you were never committed in the first place. Perhaps you were always looking for an excuse to walk away."

"You don't really believe that."

"Right now, Emily," he says, "I don't know what to believe."

"Then maybe there's nothing left for us to discuss." I shift on my feet. "Maybe you should just step aside and let me go."

"How far do you think you can run, Em?" Jack sneers, his eyes dark and unreadable. "You can't escape who you are."

"Watch me."

I am shocked that Jack doesn't put up a fight. That he does, in fact, step aside and watch me walk out.

37

Emily

My hands tremble as I grip the steering wheel, trying to ground myself with the smooth leather beneath my fingers. The city streets blur past in a dizzying kaleidoscope of colors and movement, but my mind remains fixated on that hollow click of the unloaded gun. *How did he know?* He always knows.

Panic rises in my chest, a living thing clawing to break free as I struggle to draw breath. Each turn of the wheel carries me further from the danger that I know lingers within our home, yet uncertainty clouds my vision. I have no destination in mind. There is only the primal need to escape. I don't see how we can come back from this.

A stray tear trails down my cheek as I wrestle with the implications of what I've done. Firing what I believed was a loaded gun at the man I promised to love in sickness and health. It almost feels ironic. This is definitely the sick part of that vow. Even I am amazed at the low we've managed this time.

Amid the chaos of my thoughts, a memory of Sarah's kind eyes emerges. I recall how many times she's been there, how many breakups we've seen each other through. Rachel, too, though she has Lucas, and I'd prefer that Jack not know where I am.

My hands seem to move of their own volition, steering the vehicle toward the only solace I have left. Each familiar street sign brings me closer to Sarah's front porch, a temporary refuge from the nightmare my life has become.

As I pull up outside her house, hesitation settles in my bones. What will I say when she answers the door? How can I possibly explain how bad things are? I rehearse it in my mind. But when Sarah answers the door, when her concerned face comes into view, I find the words elude me.

Her widening eyes take in my disheveled state, the tears streaking down my cheeks. In that moment, I see the questions forming on her lips, but before she can voice them, I collapse into her waiting arms. A sob racks my body as she pulls me in for a hug, her embrace a comfort I am powerless to resist.

Here in the safety of Sarah's arms, the facade I have so carefully maintained crumbles away, leaving me bare and trembling. But there is no judgment in her eyes, only a well of compassion and understanding as deep as the ocean.

"Emily, what happened?" Her voice is soft yet urgent, hands rubbing my back in soothing circles. I cling to her, the tremors racking my body as the adrenaline wears off.

Sarah guides me inside, and I settle onto the plush sofa as she disappears into the kitchen. The familiar surroundings evoke memories of happier times, a stark contrast to how I feel now.

Sarah returns moments later, pressing a mug of steaming tea into my hands. "Drink this. You'll feel better."

I nod, cradling the mug close as its warmth seeps into my palms. I take a sip, the hot liquid soothing my raw throat.

Sarah sits beside me, wrapping an arm around my shoulders. "Do you want to talk about it?"

I shake my head, fresh tears welling up at the thought of revisiting the events that drove me here. "Not yet," I say. "I just...I couldn't stay there another second. He—" My voice breaks off, throat clenching around the words I cannot bring myself to say.

Jack is going to kill me. I can't stay here, either.

"You don't have to explain," Sarah says gently. "You can stay here as long as you need."

I lay my head on Sarah's shoulder, the events of the morning finally catching up to me in a wave of bone-deep exhaustion. My eyelids droop heavily, but still I cling to wakefulness, afraid of what might happen if I give in. She nods toward the guest room.

"Rest." Sarah gives my shoulder a gentle squeeze. "I'll be here when you wake up."

38

Emily

Darkness drapes the guest room, leaving me alone with the whispers of my mind. The sheets tangle around me like constricting vines as I toss and turn, unable to escape from the gnawing doubts that plague me. *I shouldn't be here.*

Reluctantly, I force my eyes open, staring at the ceiling above. Sleep eludes me.

"Emily," Sarah's voice pierces through the haze of my thoughts, her tone cautious yet guarded. She peeks her head in the door. "You awake?"

"Uh-huh."

"Could you watch the baby for a few minutes? I need to grab the mail."

I cast a glance at her retreating figure. "Sure."

Forcing myself out of bed, I stumble groggily into the living room, where Ian is playing in his bouncy seat. I reach down and unfasten him.

"I'll just be a second," Sarah calls out, already halfway to the door.

The baby coos in my arms, his chubby fingers curling around my thumb as I stare out the window into the backyard. We stand there for several minutes as I point out the trees, a squirrel, and various birds.

A buzzing sound behind me catches my attention. My gaze drifts toward Sarah's phone, abandoned on the coffee table. As if on cue, it vibrates again with a new notification. A message from someone named "My Love."

My heart lurches, and I force myself to swallow the bile rising in my throat as I glance at the message: *How long is she going to be there??? I can't wait to see you... on your knees, that is...*

What the hell?

And then another appears on the screen: *Whatever you have to do, get rid of her.*

My heartbeat thrums in my ears. Sarah said she'd only be a minute, but it's been over ten. A floorboard creaks behind me. I whip around, clutching the baby to my chest.

Silence.

Just the house settling.

I glance at the phone again, my eyes tracing the words "My Love" scrawled across the screen.

Who the hell is My Love?

The baby gurgles, his mouth forming an O. I shush him gently, running a hand over his soft hair.

"Sarah?" I call out, trying to keep my voice steady as she slips back through the door, clutching a handful of envelopes.

"Everything all right?"

Her eyes narrow, scrutinizing my expression.

I plaster a smile on my face. "Fine."

But it's not fine. My muscles clench as I grip the baby tighter, my mind racing. Is this some twisted joke?

"Here, let me take him," she says, reaching for the baby. Her touch makes my blood run cold, and I reluctantly relinquish my hold. How could I have missed this? Had there been something about her, something off?

"Thanks," I say, watching her coo at the baby, and suddenly, I yearn for someone to confide in, someone who will listen and discount my suspicions. My thoughts drift to Rachel, and I wonder if she's noticed anything strange about Sarah.

"Emily?" Sarah interrupts my thoughts, arching a brow. "You seem...distracted."

"I haven't slept," I say with a forced smile, trying to shrug off her concern. "I should probably head home soon."

"Of course," she nods. "Marital spats always look a little clearer after a few hours, don't they?" I watch as she kisses Ian's head. "I really miss that—not the fighting—but you know…"

"I'm sorry," I say. "I shouldn't have come here."

"Are you kidding? It thrilled Ian and me to see another face. Especially yours."

"Thanks, Sarah." I lean over and caress the baby's head. "And thank you, little man."

And with that, I grab my purse and slip out of the house, my heart pounding. As soon as I'm outside, I fumble for my phone, my fingers trembling as I try to get Rachel on the phone. The line rings once, twice, three times.

Come on, pick up.

I hang up and call again. The fourth ring cuts off suddenly, and a familiar voice answers on the other end.

"Emily? What's wrong?"

"Rachel…" Relief floods through me. "We need to talk."

39

Emily

My car speeds down the highway, the world outside a blur of colors and shapes. "What is it?" Rachel says. The sound of her concerned voice is like a balm to my frayed nerves.

"I..."

"Emily, what's wrong?" There's an intuition in her tone that tells me she knows something is amiss.

"Everything is falling apart, Rach. I don't know what to do anymore." Hot tears threaten to spill over, staining my cheeks as I struggle to keep my composure.

"Is it Jack?"

Of course, it's Jack. "It's everything. Work...Will's death... everything."

"Em, it's going to be okay," she reassures me, her sincerity wrapping around me like a warm embrace. "Maybe you need to get away for a bit and regroup."

The idea of escaping, even if just for a little while, feels like a lifeline, which is maybe why I clutch at it with desperate hope. I am not ready to go home.

"Where do I go?" I ask, intrigued by the prospect of not having to face Jack, to not feel like I'm being watched every second of every day.

"You could go out to the farm. It's peaceful there..."

"I remember."

"Well then, what's stopping you?"

"I don't know. Nothing—"

"You can clear your head, focus on figuring things out. Probably catch up on work..."

"Thank you," I say, relief washing over me like a cool rain after a sweltering day.

Rachel gives me the address so I can plug it in. "Good," she says. "I'll take care of everything for your arrival. Just focus on getting there."

"Thank you, Rachel. I don't know what I'd do without you."

"Drive safely, Em. I'll see you soon."

I hang up and head to my office, where I hastily pack a bag with essential items: my laptop, a notebook, and the makeup bag in my desk drawer.

Before getting on the road, I make a quick stop at the mall to purchase some underwear, lounge wear, jeans, and a couple of pairs of shoes. Anything to avoid the daunting prospect of going home to confront Jack.

The transition from the oppressive city to the open countryside is like a balm for my soul. The car hums softly as I navigate the winding roads, flanked by verdant fields and rolling hills. A sense of trepidation mingles with excitement in my chest, each heartbeat pounding out a question: will I find the peace I seek?

Soon, the sky overhead stretches wide and blue, dotted with fluffy white clouds that seem to beckon me onward. This new landscape offers a soothing contrast to the turmoil that has consumed my life in recent weeks, and I find myself feeling grateful for Rachel's suggestion.

As I approach the farm, the scent of freshly cut grass and earthy fields envelops me, further immersing me in the idyllic haven. My heart swells with nostalgia at the sight of the charming farmhouse, its weathered walls and creaking porch promising solace.

"Emily, you made it!" Rachel's warm embrace greets me as I step out of the car. Her genuine concern, evident in her furrowed brow and soft eyes, ground me. "I'm so glad you're here."

"Thank you for inviting me," I say. "I don't know what I would do without you."

Her eyes crinkle at the corners. "Hey, that's what friends are for."

"No, seriously. I've forgotten how perfect this place is. Thank you."

"Of course," she says, squeezing my hand reassuringly. "I hope you're not mad, but I've got to head back to the city."

"Oh—"

Rachel frowns. "I know. I was hoping for some girl time, too."

"It's fine."

"I'll be back in a few days," she says. "But let me show you around first."

40

Anonymous

The winding country road stretches endlessly before me. My heart pounds, fueled by a volatile mixture of dread, anticipation, and morbid curiosity.

I swallow hard, glancing at the rearview mirror. Not a soul behind me as far as the eye can see, just me and the lush green hills that line the sides of the narrow stretch.

The picturesque scenery of rolling hills and green fields should calm me. Instead, a tense coil of unease winds tighter in the pit of my stomach with each mile marker I pass.

How did I end up here chasing her? One thing you should know, never trust anyone who is always running. It leads nowhere good.

I swallow around the lump in my throat, blinking back the anticipation. No time for that now. I have a purpose, a mission to fulfill.

The weathered sign for Blackwood Farm comes into view, its

peeling paint a silent welcome. My hands clench around the steering wheel as I turn onto the gravel driveway, rocks crunching under the tires.

What an interesting place, and how very predictable.

The old farmhouse looms before me, shrouded in shadows as twilight approaches. An owl hoots in the distance, bidding farewell to the light. The last vestiges of daylight fade behind the house, cloaking the dilapidated barn and rusty silos in the darkness.

I pull off the road and kill the engine, and silence falls around me, broken only by the ticking of the cooling engine. So, this is where everything begins and ends. I step out of the car, excited, gravel grinding under my shoes, and stand there, a smile and the sun upon my face as I consider my next move.

41

Emily

The crickets' chorus serenades the night as I rest on the front porch of Rachel's farmhouse, their song mingling with the distant sound of a dog barking. My laptop lays open on my lap, its screen casting an eerie glow that dances with the fireflies flickering around me. The details of Will's murder surround me like a shroud, refusing to let go.

I dial Rachel's number, my fingers trembling slightly as I press the phone against my ear. She answers, her voice warm and familiar, like a favorite blanket.

"Hey, Em, is everything okay?"

"I've been thinking about something…" I hesitate, biting my lip. "It's crazy to even say… I mean, I know…"

She sighs like she knows what I'm about to say. "You sound tired, Em."

"I know. But I just can't get it out of my mind." I sigh and decide to just spit it out. "Do you think Sarah could have been involved in Will's death?"

"What?" Rachel snaps. "Emily—do you even hear yourself?"

"Yeah—"

"We're talking about *Sarah*. Meek little Sarah?" Rachel says. "I know how much seeing Will like that is affecting you—it's affecting all of us," she says, "But you can't keep torturing yourself. It's not healthy."

I swallow hard, blinking away tears. "Maybe you're right." The weight of doubt settles across my shoulders. "But something doesn't feel right. There are too many unanswered questions, and I can't shake this feeling that we're missing something important."

"Emily, hon, you're not a detective, and you're only going to make things worse by stirring up trouble. I think it's best if you leave the investigation to the police."

I swallow hard, trying to ignore the nagging suspicion that claws at my insides. My gaze flits back to the laptop screen, the unsolved puzzle taunting me. I wonder if my desperation has blinded me. "I can't stop thinking about it. About him just lying there with a knife in his neck, Rach."

"Em, it's late." Rachel's voice is gentle but firm. "You should get some rest. What's that saying? Don't borrow trouble?"

"I know, and I hear you but—"

"You can't just go around accusing people without any evidence, Em. Sarah is our friend, and she's going through hell right now."

Her reaction catches me off guard, and for a moment, I'm speechless. Her words sting more than I expect.

"Sorry, you're right," I say, rubbing my temple, as if that might ease the weight of everything. "I'm just trying to make sense of it, is all."

"I'm worried about you, Em." Rachel sighs, her anger replaced with concern. "You need to focus on yourself right now—have you spoken to Jack?"

"No, not yet."

"Hmmm."

"Please make sure Lucas doesn't tell him I'm here, okay?"

"If that's what you want…"

"It is," I say. "I just need time to think."

Rachel and I exchange a few more words before hanging up, but her final sentiment sticks with me. I stare at the night sky, trying to figure out my next move. The fireflies' glow wanes, and the darkness of the night seems to press in on me.

Should I call Jack?

I shudder, the sudden realization hitting me like a freight train as I recall Jack's peculiar question during our argument—did Michael stop by our home? The memory dances at the edge of my consciousness, teasing me with its significance.

Michael. My fingers drum on the laptop as I chew my lip. *Why would Jack ask about Michael?* He'd never shown much fondness for our chef before. Did he suspect Michael? Or was he merely concerned for my mental well-being, wanting someone around so I wouldn't be alone?

No. There has to be more to it than that. Jack is hiding something from me…

My gut twists in a thousand different directions as my fingers fly over the keyboard, searching for any shred of information on Michael. Each click leads me further into the labyrinth of possibilities. But, unfortunately, to nothing concrete. I can't find much on Michael at all, other than a one-page personal website about his business. But then, I feel ridiculous, and possibly a little like Rachel inferred— crazy. What reason would Michael have for wanting Will dead?

I slam the laptop shut.

Damn it. What am I missing? Which crucial piece of the puzzle can't I see?

"Will," I say, staring out into the night. "Who wanted you dead?"

The question hangs heavy in the air. Neither answered nor willing to fade away until the whirr of tires on gravel down the road draws my attention. When I look up, I'm surprised to see Ava's car pull up the drive. Her unexpected arrival offers a welcome distraction from my own spiraling thoughts. It feels good not to be alone.

"Emily," she says, climbing out of her car, enveloping me in a tight hug. "I thought you might want some company."

"Rachel sent you."

"Ummm," Ava scrunches up her nose. "Not exactly."

"Then how'd you know I was here?"

"Okay, fine," she huffs. "It was Rach."

I roll my eyes. "Can't say I'm shocked."

After I've helped Ava collect her things and we head into the house, she breaks out a bottle of wine and pours two glasses. "I brought the good stuff," she says as I relay my conversation with Rachel.

She nods in agreement as she hands me a glass. "Rachel's right," she says. "You're too close to this, Em. Let the cops do their job. They'll figure it out."

"Only fifty-one percent of homicides in the US are ever solved…"

Ava gives me a look.

"What?" I say, gulping my wine. "I've done my research…"

"Yeah, that might be the problem."

There's a long, pressing silence that neither of us seems eager to fill. "Maybe you're both right," I admit, feeling a pang of self-doubt.

Ava shifts in her seat. "I take it things with Jack aren't going too well?"

"We just need a break from each other," I say. "You know how it is—"

Instantly, I wish I could roll the words back into my mouth

and keep it shut. Bringing up anything about relationships when Ava is drinking is a recipe for disaster.

"Yeah..." Ava finishes her glass and pours another. "But I've never really trusted Jack. And I know you two have had your issues."

"What married couple doesn't?"

"But think about it..." Ava leans forward, her eyes narrowed and calculating. "He's always been secretive, hasn't he? Maybe he knows something he isn't telling you." She looks away and then back at me. "We all know he and Will had their troubles..."

"Stop it, Ava." I shake my head, but her insinuations slither through my mind, taking root like parasitic vines. "Jack wouldn't do that..."

"Who knows?" Ava shrugs, a strange smile playing at the corners of her lips. "But maybe it's worth considering."

42

Emily

My eyes flutter open as the first morning light filters through the farmhouse windows. For a moment, I'm disoriented, confused about my surroundings. Then memories of last night flood back—sitting in the kitchen with Ava, her suggestions about Jack.

I rub the sleep from my eyes, a dull ache forming behind them. I don't recall having more than one glass of wine, but it feels as though I downed an entire bottle.

I ease myself out of bed and pad downstairs on bare feet, the wooden floorboards creaking under each step. Ava is already awake, standing at the stove and scrambling eggs in a cast-iron skillet. The savory aroma wafts through the kitchen, but my stomach churns at the thought of food.

Ava glances up as I enter the room, her brow furrowing with concern. "Morning. I thought you could use a good breakfast after last night. Feeling any better?"

I give a noncommittal shrug and lean against the counter. "Not really."

"Em..." Ava trails off with a sigh. I can tell she wants to continue our conversation from last night, but when she takes a second glance at me, she thinks better of it.

After a moment, she simply says, "I've got to head back soon. But I thought I'd make us breakfast first."

"Thank you."

"Just promise me you'll take care of yourself, okay?"

I muster up a weak smile. "I will. Don't worry about me."

It's a hollow reassurance, and we both know it. Ava slides the eggs onto two plates and we sit down to eat, the tension hanging thick in the air between us. I take a bite so not to appear rude, but then spend the rest of the time pushing the eggs around on my plate with my fork.

"I thought you'd be hungry..."

"I'm a little hungover," I say, feeling dizzy. My unease is mirrored in the frown tugging at the corners of Ava's lips. *Had I said something last night?* I can't recall.

Ava finishes up her breakfast quickly. I watch as she straightens the kitchen and makes an equally hasty exit.

I don't even wait for her to pull off onto the main road before I give Detective Alvarez a call.

My heart thuds like a hummingbird's wings against my chest when he answers, his tone gruff and professional. "Detective Alvarez," he says, "how can I help you?"

"Hi, it's me, Emily." I swallow hard, emboldened by the memory of Will's confession in the garden. "Emily Brown."

"Yes?"

"I have some information about the murder case you're working on."

"Go on," he replies, his tone changing to sound encouraging.

I share what I know, and he listens intently. When I finish, he asks if we can meet in person. "I'm visiting a friend out of town," I say. "I should be back in the city in a few days. Can I call you then?"

"Of course."

As the call ends, a glimmer of optimism courses through me—my explanation of events might remove any hints of suspicion from me—or Jack. But the uneasiness lingers, unanswered questions circling like vultures above a carcass. The weight of betraying Sarah gnaws at me, but I must fix this, whatever the cost.

43

Emily

The creaking floorboards betray Rachel's arrival, and my heart clenches as her footsteps echo through the old farmhouse. My gut churns with a cocktail of anticipation and dread, knowing all too well that her presence means I'll be forced to return to the city sooner than I'd hoped. I can't hide out here forever, and it's only a matter of time before she brings it up. I know she's worried about my mental state, hence her reason for sending Ava, and coming back early.

"Hey," I say, swallowing hard as I descend the stairs.

"Em, you look awful."

My nausea has little to do with the hangover gnawing at me. "Yeah, I'm not feeling too hot."

"Rough night?" Rachel inquires, her eyebrows arching in an all-too-familiar gesture. She steps into the kitchen, each footfall stirring up a storm of emotions within me.

"Something like that," I say, avoiding her gaze. "I'm sorry, but I think I need to lie down."

"Sure, go ahead," she says, her voice softening with concern. "I plan on staying the night."

With a weak nod, I shuffle toward the stairs, my legs feeling as though they're made of lead. Each step seems to sap what little energy I have left, but I force myself to continue upward. The bedroom offers little solace, its tranquility serving as a stark contrast to the chaos churning inside me.

As I close the door, my stomach lurches, and I stagger over to the bed. The world spins around me as I collapse onto the mattress, desperate for a moment of respite. Time stretches on, a distorted symphony of Rachel moving about the house and distant birdsong accompanying my troubled thoughts.

My fingers fumble for my phone, desperate for the comfort it brings.

I will myself to fall asleep. But no matter how hard I try, I can't shake this feeling that something is terribly wrong.

I close my eyes, Rachel's footsteps echoing in the back of my mind. When I open them again and reach out blindly for my phone, a jolt of panic surges within me as I switch it on and see Jack's flurry of missed calls.

My heart drops when I read the notification — one email saying all too much. It's official: I'm fired.

The realization washes over me, and suddenly the room feels like it's spinning. All I want is the energy to stand up, but heavy fatigue takes hold of me, and all I can do is lay back down into oblivion.

I squeeze my eyes shut, praying for sleep to return, but my mind and my stomach continues to churn. Rachel's presence downstairs gives me a little comfort; at least if I pass out, I'm not alone.

The low drone of her voice reaches up to me, like a swarm of bees on a summer day. I want to block it out, but curiosity nags at me, tugging relentlessly at my composure.

My limbs tremble as I get out of bed and make my way to the door, the floorboards groaning beneath me like the moans of a dying man. I hesitate, my heart pounding in my chest, then clamber down the stairs with fear biting at my ankles.

"Of course, you're worried about her," Rachel says, an emotion coloring her voice that I can't quite name. "But it's not your fault she's losing it. And Will never stood a chance." Her words are bitter and hollow. "It was only a matter of time before—"

The person on the other end of the line utters something that sparks an exasperated sigh from Rachel.

"What does it even matter?" she snaps back. "What's done is done."

"Still what?" Rachel interjects sharply. "I'm not saying it will be easy, but we have to face facts."

My heart races as I press against the banister, straining to hear more.

"Look," Rachel says in a softer voice, almost like she's trying to make amends. "Sometimes we have to make tough choices."

"It's done. Sarah… Will had it coming, hon… you know what he put you through. We did the right thing."

"Don't cry, sweetheart. I love you too much…I'm gonna figure out a way to fix this…"

The weight of Rachel's words hit me full force. Oh God. Sarah didn't just have a lover.

She had an accomplice.

44

Emily

The stairs creak beneath me and suddenly Rachel spins on her heels, her eyes locking on mine. "Emily."

With the tap of the button, and without a goodbye, she ends the call. My eyes remain fixed on hers, searching for signs of remorse or denial.

"Em, I don't know what you think you heard, but—"

Her words falter under the weight of my stare.

My voice emerges from within me, laced with anger and vulnerability, echoing in the air between us. "You owe me an explanation."

"Unfortunately," she breathes out, her voice cracking, "it's not that simple."

Rachel's eyes widen, and her face contorts with a mix of panic and fury. She clenches her jaw, her gaze shifting from me to the door behind me. I can almost see the gears turning in her head as she calculates her options, the desperation in her eyes betraying her fear.

"Rachel," I warn.

But before I can react further, Rachel grabs a hammer from the bar and lunges forward, her attack swift and merciless. The hammer collides with my cheek, sending a shockwave of pain through my skull. My world erupts into chaos as the blows land.

"Stop!" I cry out, raising my arms to shield myself from her relentless assault.

Desperation fuels Rachel's movements. Her face is twisted with a rage I've never seen before. It's as if she's been hiding it all this time, just beneath the surface, waiting for the right moment to unleash it.

I fight back with a ferocity I didn't know I possessed, pushing her away and landing a solid kick to her stomach. She doubles over, gasping for breath, but I don't give her time to recover.

My eyes dart between the door and the kitchen, but even if I make it out, I don't have my keys. So, I turn for the kitchen, searching for a knife, for any weapon that will suffice.

I do not make it very far before the taste of iron fills my mouth, a metallic bitterness that lingers on my tongue. Gasping for air, I stagger backward, my hand instinctively seeking the source of the searing pain in my side. It comes away slick with blood.

"Rach?" I choke out, struggling to make sense of what is happening. My vision swims, blurring the edges of the room until all I can focus on is Rachel's heaving chest and wild eyes. She has quite literally stabbed me in the back,

"Em... I'm sorry," she whispers, her voice raw with desperation. But there's something else in her eyes, something harder, colder. A determination that wasn't there before.

"You're sorry?" I spit through gritted teeth, using the wall behind me for support as I try to rise. The effort sends a fresh wave of agony radiating through my body, but I refuse to let it break me. I won't give Rachel the satisfaction of seeing me fall.

"I didn't want any of this. I just wanted to protect you."

"Protect me?" I echo incredulously. "By attacking me? By lying and manipulating me? If this is your idea of protection, I'd hate to see what you consider a betrayal…" I suck a deep breath in. "Oh, wait."

As I press my palm to the wound to stop the bleeding, I scan the area for the knife because wherever it is, it isn't in Rachel's hand. She's gripping the hammer.

"Em, I…" she falters, the words dying in her throat.

Rachel lunges for me, but I sidestep her grasp, using every ounce of energy I have left to keep my distance.

"Emily, please," she sobs, her hand reaching out as if to bridge the gap between us.

"I don't want to hurt you," she says, but that turns out to be a lie like everything else.

With one swing, the hammer connects with my ribs, and then I feel nothing.

Silence settles over the room like a suffocating blanket, broken only by my ragged gasps for air. I lay there on the wooden floor, battered and broken, my body screaming in protest, my blood a testament to the price I've paid for not turning around and creeping back up those stairs. I should have let it be. I should have pretended I heard nothing, saw nothing.

"You never did know when to leave well enough alone," Rachel says.

My mind races, searching desperately for any glimmer of hope, any semblance of a plan that could get me out of this house. I have to be smart if I want to survive. Rachel isn't just going to let me go. She has every reason to kill me. She just said as much on the phone.

I know I should stay put, but the possibility of bleeding to death feels somehow beneath me. I didn't come this far to die like this.

With a steely resolve, I force myself up onto shaky legs, gritting my teeth against the pain that flares anew. Every muscle screams its protest, but I ignore them, focusing instead on the adrenaline coursing through my veins.

"Rachel," I say, lunging at her. "You won't win this."

Her eyes widen in surprise, and then everything goes black.

45

Anonymous

The acrid stench of Emily's urine and feces assaults my senses as I ascend the stairs into the bedroom. My stomach churns at the smell, but I ignore the unpleasantness, focusing instead on the sounds of Emily's pained whimpers drifting up from the darkness above.

With each step, anticipation builds within me, my pulse quickening at the thought of tormenting her and finishing her off. By the time I reach the top of the stairs, a sadistic glee surges through my veins, craving the sight of Emily's battered body and the sounds of her anguished cries.

She's huddled in the far corner of the room, her broken foot twisted at an unnatural angle. The contusions mottling her pale skin stand as a testament to my merciless aggression.

"Please..." Emily rasps, her voice hoarse from screaming. "I can't take any more."

Her plea elicits a sharp pang of arousal, followed swiftly by a surge of triumph. Emily clings to the frayed edges of her resilience, her spirit shattering beneath the weight of my torment.

With slow, deliberate steps, I cross the bedroom, relishing the panic that flickers in her eyes. Each movement sends a jolt of pain through her broken body, and by the time I reach her, she is trembling, her breaths coming in ragged gasps.

Kneeling beside her, I caress the bruises on her cheek, tracing the damage I've inflicted. "You were always so pretty," I whisper, my fingers tightening around Emily's jaw. "I hate to see you like this."

A strangled sob escapes her throat as the full implications of my claim sink in. Her fate is now in my hands, her life and death subject to my whims.

She stares at me with dead, hollow eyes that speak of a spirit broken beyond repair. Her silence satisfies me more than any scream or plea, a sign of her utter surrender.

"The problem, you see, was that my parents never let me have any pets..."

The thought elicits a surge of arousal. My fingers tighten in Emily's hair, and I crush my lips against hers, tasting blood and defeat. She remains unresponsive, a rag doll in my grasp, but it hardly diminishes my pleasure.

I release her from my grasp, admiring the bruises that mar her pale skin. My mark of ownership, proof of her captivity. Em curls into herself, clutching her broken ribs, the movement eliciting a pained whimper. The sound causes my lips to curve into a predatory smile.

"On your knees," I command, eager to demonstrate my dominance once more.

Her eyes gleam with fear, but she remains motionless, defiance flickering behind her gaze. Rage bubbles up inside me at her insolence. Once again, I seize a fistful of her hair and wrench her head back, relishing her strangled cry.

"You will obey me," I hiss, "or you will suffer. The choice is entirely yours." I punctuate the threat with a brutal backhand, splitting Emily's lip. Blood trickles down her chin as she moves onto her knees with a sob.

Triumph lights my eyes as I tower over Em's cowering form. She is broken, in body and spirit, but still needs reminding of her place.

I watch the realization dawn in her eyes. The fight has left her, extinguished by the hopelessness of her plight.

"Good girl," I croon, fisting my hand in her hair once more. "That's what you like, isn't it? Dominance?" I can't help but smile. "I saw you with Will—and I wasn't the only one."

She refuses me the dignity of a response, which is so Emily. Prideful, always. That's what landed her in this position in the first place.

"You didn't fight back today," I purr, my tone a mocking caress. She shudders, curling into an even tighter ball. I smile, relishing her reaction. "Perhaps I will grant you a reprieve, allow your wounds to heal before we resume our delightful games."

Emily peers up at me through a tangled veil of hair, eyes gleaming with terror and hope in equal measure. I reach out to brush a stray lock of hair from her cheek, then I grasp her chin, forcing her to meet my gaze.

"Fret not, my pet. As soon as the hole is dug, this will all be over."

I release her abruptly and stand, turning on my heel. Her ragged sobs fade into the distance as I descend the stairs, my lips curled into a triumphant smirk. The game is far from over, but for now, I am satisfied.

46

Emily

I survey the farmhouse bedroom, its eerie vibes heightened by the pale yellow wallpaper clinging to the walls like decaying flesh. Dust motes twirl in the faint sunlight coming through the dirty window.

My breaths come shallow and rapid, each one a futile attempt to fill my lungs with the stale air that suffocates me. The sensation of drowning intensifies as I take in the oppressive atmosphere—the heavy curtains that shroud the room in darkness, the rusted iron bed frame that looms over me, and the peeling paint on the ceiling that resembles gnarled, twisted fingers reaching down to grasp my throat.

"Quite a charming place you have here," I say.

She smirks, her cold eyes reflecting the sinister glow of the room. "Why, thank you, Emily. I've always been a fan of ambiance."

"Your phone," she taunts, waving the device in front of me like a sadistic puppeteer. "You won't be needing it."

Trapped like a wounded animal, I can't stifle the chilling realization of my captivity, tightening its grip on my already fragile composure. Yet, beneath the fear and despair, a burning ember of defiance refuses to be extinguished. I will not let this be the end; I will find a way out of this.

As she speaks, I can't help but notice the way her fingers dance gracefully across the back of an antique armchair, as if orchestrating the symphony of deception that is unfolding around us.

"Anyhow, I'm back for story time."

"I'm not in the mood."

"Ah, but Em," she says. "You've always loved girl talk."

"Fine." I glance toward the window, knowing that the longer she talks, the greater the odds that someone will find me here. I just can't let her know that. "But just know, nothing you have to say is of any interest to me."

"Oh, but I beg to differ. Did you know Will was planning to leave Sarah for another woman?" Her voice slithers through the air like smoke, her words laced with venom. "Of course you didn't. But Sarah knew, and I made sure she understood just how much of a snake he was."

I feel my heart clench painfully in my chest, its rhythm stuttering as I try to comprehend the depths of her deceit. My eyes follow her every movement, tracking the predatory sway of her hips, the sinister glint in her eyes. She's not the friend I thought I knew; she's exactly what Jack tried to tell me she was, a snake.

"Once Sarah realized how little she meant to Will, it didn't take much to convince her she deserved better."

Her laughter chills me to the bone, a sound devoid of warmth or compassion. "And I was all too happy to help her see the truth."

"Help her?" I say, my voice trembling with barely contained fury. "What you mean is you manipulated her, twisted her thoughts until she couldn't see any other way out."

She has always loved talking about herself.

"Isn't it fascinating how easily the human mind can be swayed?" she muses, her voice soft and dangerous. "With just the right combination of lies and half-truths, I created a monster out of Will. She believed he was abusing her—emotionally, if not physically. And eventually, she decided it was time to make him pay."

"By killing him."

"Exactly," she confirms, her eyes gleaming with a sick satisfaction. "Sarah only managed to inflict a single wound," she says, leaning back against the doorframe with a chilling smile. "But it was enough to weaken him."

"I don't want to hear this. Will was our friend."

"No. Will was your fuck buddy—and that's different."

"We only had sex once."

She shakes her head. "And your point is?"

"I don't want to talk about this."

"So what?" she quips. "You're not going anywhere, and it's too hot for me to keep digging your hole… How else are we supposed to fill the time?"

"Anyway—Sarah's pathetic attempt was enough for me to finish the job." The words hang heavy in the air, and I feel my blood run cold.

"Then why deny it to Sarah? Why lie to her and pretend you weren't involved?" My voice quivers as I ask the question, my hands clenching into fists on the bedspread. "You made her think it was all her fault…"

"Because, Emily, dear," she says, "I'm a master manipulator, remember? I need people like Sarah under my control. And if she thinks she's the only guilty party… Well, that gives me power over her."

Her grin is malicious, twisted, and I shudder involuntarily.

"You're sick," I say, glaring at her with every ounce of hatred I possess. "You used your best friend, manipulated her into committing murder, just so you could feel powerful."

"Exactly." A grin spreads across her face. "Plus, she's great in bed. I mean, who would've thought?"

"How do you live with yourself?"

"Quite easily, actually." Her eyes narrow in amusement. "I've always been good at compartmentalizing. Besides, Sarah needed someone to show her the way."

She tilts her head, studying me. "And now, so do you."

"You're mistaken," I say. "I will never let you control me."

"We'll see," she sighs. "Anyway, your precious Sarah and I have been seeing each other for two years now. Bet you didn't know that…"

Her gaze never leaves mine, the triumph in her eyes undeniable.

"Two years?" *How could I have been so blind?*

"So it was you texting her to get rid of me."

"Yep. But stop interrupting!" She rolls her eyes. "What I was saying was—we've had two beautiful, passionate years," she continues, her voice dripping with satisfaction. "Sarah was always too good for Will, you know. He never deserved someone as sensitive and loving as her. And you were so good at playing the victim, Em. Sarah's so gullible…"

I struggle to wrap my head around it all, the web of deceit that has been right in front of my face all along.

"You didn't really think she'd choose him over me, did you?" She scoffs at the idea. "You and Jack were nothing more than pawns in our game."

"Game?" I shift on the bed, wincing. "You call this a game?"

"Isn't it?" She smirks, leaning back against the dresser, her hands resting on her hips. "Life is just one big chessboard, Emily. And we're all just pieces, waiting to be moved."

"I suppose it's easy if you're the one controlling the board."

"Isn't that always the way?" She shrugs. "The powerful prey on the weak, exploiting their vulnerabilities until they're under their thumb?"

"Why are you telling me all this? Why not just keep me locked up here, in the dark?"

"Because, my dear Emily," she says, her tone condescending and venomous. "Like I told you—it's hot out, and I'm not finished digging your grave."

47

Emily

"Sarah wasn't as innocent as you believe," she says, shaking me awake. "She was desperate to escape Will's grasp, and I simply provided her with the means to do so."

"By convincing her to kill him—you've said that."

My heart races, anger boiling beneath the surface. My broken foot throbs mercilessly, and I just want to sleep, but she won't allow it.

"Sarah knew what she was getting into," she snaps. "I didn't force her to do anything. She wanted to be with me, to be free from that pathetic excuse for a husband."

"Sarah's resistance only fueled your obsession," I accuse, my words slicing through the air like a knife. "You couldn't stand the thought of her slipping away, of losing control over her."

It's the same reason she won't let me sleep. This, and she doesn't want to be alone with herself.

"Control is everything, Emily," she says. "When you have

someone wrapped around your finger, you can make them do anything you want."

The gravity of the situation settles in. "Even murder."

"Especially murder," she confirms, a wicked smile gracing her lips. "The ultimate display of devotion, don't you think?"

"Devotion? You're delusional. That isn't love; it's coercion."

My thoughts race to Jack, my chest aching with the weight of the truth. "But Sarah will realize that eventually, and when she does, your twisted world will come crumbling down."

"Is that a threat, Em?" she smirks, her eyes glinting wickedly. "You're in no position to make those."

"Maybe not now," I say, my resolve unwavering. "But one day, you'll get what's coming to you. People always do."

I close my eyes, eager to drift off. "And whether I'm around to see it makes no difference."

"Bold words for a caged bird," she says before leaving me alone with my thoughts, the door slamming shut behind her. Finally, I can get some sleep.

48

Anonymous

The low rumble of an engine approaches the farmhouse, shattering the eerie silence that has held us captive. Peering through a crack in the curtains, I watch the unmarked car pull into the driveway, my stomach twisting into knots.

"Emily," I call out, my voice strained. "We have company. One word and you're dead."

I can't help but shiver as I step outside, my eyes landing on the fresh hell this situation has brought now. The eeriness of the farm seems to heighten with his arrival, casting an ominous shadow over the entire place.

The wind kicks up as Detective Alvarez steps out of the car, his footsteps crunching on the gravel driveway.

"Hello?" he calls out, his voice steady, but a hint of apprehension lacing his tone.

"Detective." I force a smile onto my lips. "What brings you all the way out here?"

"May I come in? I need to speak with Emily," he says, and I can sense his unease as he scans the surroundings.

"Of course, please." I step aside to let him enter.

As the detective steps inside, the haunting atmosphere wraps around him like a suffocating embrace. He scans the surroundings, his eyes narrowed and senses on high alert, taking in every unsettling detail with a practiced gaze.

Cold sweat trickles down my spine as I lead him toward the bedroom. The creaking floorboards beneath our feet seem to amplify the sickening weight of my lies. My pulse races, and I taste bile at the back of my throat. This isn't part of the plan.

"Emily's in here." I push the bedroom door open with a trembling hand. The detective steps inside, his eyes widening at the sight of Emily, battered and bruised, like a fragile bird with clipped wings. A pitiful creature.

"Jesus," he says, concern etching lines across his face. As he moves closer to her, I see his assumption forming a dark cloud of doubt about Jack. I am more than happy to let him indulge this suspicion. It's like he's manifesting the lies for me.

"Who did this?" Detective Alvarez asks, his voice soft yet steady, like that of a priest taking confession. Emily's eyes dart between him and me, fear shimmering within their depths.

I give her a slight nod, and a wicked thrill surges through me. This power, this control over another person—it's intoxicating. I watch as Emily swallows hard and looks away from me, summoning some shred of courage before she speaks.

"Rachel... She's holding me hostage," Emily blurts out, her voice cracking.

Emily's confession lingers in the air like the stale, suffocating scent of a long-buried secret. Her eyes, once clouded with fear, now shimmer with an ember of defiance. Detective Alvarez regards her with a mix of concern and disbelief, his gaze shifting from Emily to me.

Tears stream down Emily's cheeks. "Please... help me."

Her words hang heavy in the air, a dangerous revelation threatening to unravel everything.

"Rachel," Alvarez starts, but I cut him off, my pulse quickening like a cornered animal.

"Detective, you have no reason to believe her," I say, my words venomous and desperate. But even as I say them, I can feel the walls closing in around me.

I watch as his hand drifts slowly to the gun on his hip. His fingers curl around its handle like a lover's caress, and that's when it happens—the tipping point that changes everything.

My mask slips away like sand through an hourglass, revealing my true nature in a chilling instant. Rage surges through me, hot and uncontrollable, a wildfire consuming everything in its path. I reach for the gun in my waistband, my grip tightening around the cold metal handle.

In a single, violent motion, I aim the gun at Detective Alvarez. His eyes widen in terror as Emily screams out behind him. A malicious grin spreads across my face. "Sorry, Detective, but you shouldn't have come here."

The gun explodes with deafening ferocity, the bullet tearing through his chest. It's nice to watch the truth die with him, sinking into the silent room.

The weight of what I've done slams down on me, and I drop the gun to the floor.

For fuck's sake, now I have to dig two graves. "Emily," I snap, "this is on you."

49

Jack

The air clings to my skin like the secrets I'm certain this farm holds, my boots squelching into the mud as I follow the trail of broken footprints. The scent of death and sorrow wafts through the atmosphere, a drastic contrast to the idyllic paradise that Emily once described.

A sudden gust of wind catches me off guard, ruffling the tall grass that lines the path. Halting mid-stride, I close my eyes and listen intently to the eerie silence that surrounds me. There is no sign of life, only the faint sound of my engine cooling, ticking in rhythm with the thumping of my heart.

"Jack?" A voice cuts through the stillness, causing me to jolt backward. My gaze shifts toward Rachel, standing a few feet away, her arms folded defensively over her chest. Her eyes are hard as they stare into mine, a mixture of anger and fear swirling within their depths. She wears dirty gardening gloves and is covered in dirt, but I know for sure Rachel isn't really gardening.

"Where is she?"

"Emily?" Rachel feigns innocence, her lips curling up into a cruel smirk. "How should I know?"

"Cut the shit, Rachel." I take a menacing step forward. "I know she's here. Lucas told me. And I swear to God, if you've hurt her in any way…"

Rachel raises an eyebrow in challenge. "Or what?"

I spin around and start toward the house with Rachel hot on my heels.

"Jack, Jack, Jack…" Rachel sighs dramatically, shaking her head in mock pity. "You really think you can just waltz in here and play the hero? Did it ever cross your mind that maybe she doesn't want to see you?"

"Did it cross yours that I don't care?" Rage simmers beneath my skin as I march up to the front door and fling it open with sheer force.

The air is still and oppressive with the promise of violence. The trees seemed to sway in anticipation, their leafless branches reaching out like menacing fingers.

"Fine," Rachel says, her voice thick with challenge. "Don't take my word for it. But don't be surprised when you don't like what you find."

I spin around, anger surging through me like wildfire. "What have you done?"

She just looks at me, smiles sadly, and then shrugs. "Em doesn't want to be found, Jack. Why can't you get that through your thick skull?"

Her words are barely a whisper on the breeze, but they light a flame within me, propelling me into action. "Emily!"

With a furious intensity, I bound up the stairs to the door on the right, Rachel's footsteps close behind me. When I push open the door, darkness engulfs us and chills run up my spine at the wave of dread emanating from the room—it almost seems alive.

And there, on the bed, is Emily—a shell of her former self. Her state tears at my heart, and I feel my hands curling into fists.

"She did this to you?"

Emily's expression is tortured, and tears glisten in her eyes. Suddenly, I feel the cold metal of a gun barrel pressed into the base of my skull. With lightning speed, I spin around and pluck the gun from her hands, using the butt of it to knock her in the head.

Rachel lunges with a snarl, and our bodies slam together in a brutal, one-sided fight. She's no match for my strength and soon she knows it. Every strike brings the sweet taste of justice closer—an intoxication that only fuels my anger.

Rachel's eyes are wide with terror as she realizes her fate. My hands move to her throat as I take advantage of the moment and grip her soft flesh.

"Did you really think you'd get away with this?" My voice is low and guttural, distorted by rage.

"Jack... please..." Her words come out as desperate gasps. But I'm not letting up—there will be no mercy for her.

"Stop... please..."

In one final blow, I squeeze the life from Rachel until her once-bright eyes fade to a dull gray. The room falls silent as if mourning what has happened here.

"Emily," I say hoarsely as exhaustion sets in, replacing the anticipation of victory that had filled me moments earlier. My wife stares back at me with red-rimmed eyes, tear drops silently cascading down her cheeks. It's a sight that shocks me—there's very little I'm surprised by these days—but this...this is different.

My hands shake as I frantically untie the ropes binding Emily's fragile frame. Her eyes, those beautiful green eyes that have always grounded me, meet mine, and a flicker of relief shines through the pain.

My heart pounds so loud it drowns out everything else, but I force myself to stay calm as I dial 911. "I need an ambulance," I tell the operator.

Emily rasps my name, and I struggle for something to say—something reassuring or comforting, but she cuts me off before I can speak. "I'm so sorry."

"There's nothing to be sorry for." I smile despite the churning in my gut. "I'd do anything for you, Em. You know that."

Tears well in her eyes. "I know."

Eventually, the distant wail of sirens grows louder, weaving through the air like a lifeline.

"Everything's going to be okay, Em." I hold her close as the world comes crashing back in.

Soon the sirens reach a crescendo outside, and after that there's no time to think. Everything moves quickly. I am forced out of the room as paramedics assess my wife. Police officers arrive, just one or two at first, and then dozens.

Later, the scent of damp earth and the sharp tang of disinfectant assault my nostrils as a paramedic guides me into the back of the ambulance. I shake off his helping hand—I don't need it, not when Emily's still so fragile beside me.

"Careful there, buddy," the paramedic says, his voice gruff with concern. "You've been through a lot today."

"Jack..." Emily's fingers reach for mine. I force myself to unclench my fists, taking her hand into my own. Her touch is cold and clammy, and I worry we are far from out of the woods.

"Everything will be fine, Em." I press my lips to her hand. We both know it's a lie, but it's one I'll tell a thousand times if it gives her any comfort.

"Listen," the paramedic starts, hesitating for a moment before continuing. "I know you're worried about your wife, but we're going to take good care of her, okay?"

"Promise me something, Jack," Emily says, her eyes searching mine.

"Anything."

"Promise me you won't leave."

"I won't leave."

"Good." She manages a weak smile, her eyes fluttering closed as the paramedic adjusts her IV. "I love you."

"Love you too, Em."

It turns out only one of those things is the truth. The police do not allow me to ride in the ambulance with her. They find a cop's body, and they need me for questioning.

50

Emily

The sterile scent of disinfectant and the soft beeping of machines surround me as I sit in the hospital bed, the sunlight filtering through the blinds, casting fragmented shadows on the cold floor. My body feels fragile, still reeling from my ordeal, while the emotional scars cling to my heart like a stubborn stain.

When Jack enters the room, the sight of him fills my chest with an overwhelming mixture of love and doubt. The memories of our life together threaten to drown me, and uncertainty gnaws at the edges of my mind.

"Hey, Em," he says, his voice a soothing balm amid the chaos of my emotions. His eyes, usually guarded, soften as they meet mine. "How are you feeling?"

"Like I've been hit by a truck." I force a weak smile. "And I lived to tell about it."

He pulls a chair closer to the bed, settling down and reaching for my hand. The warmth of his touch stirs up a whirlpool of conflicting emotions within me, yet I can't bring myself to pull away.

"Em, I promise you," he says, squeezing my hand for extra emphasis, "I'm not going anywhere. And things will be different."

As I stare into his eyes, searching for any hint of deception, I find only sincerity and determination.

"I know."

"Lucas was arrested last night. Sarah, too."

"Lucas?"

"As far as charges go, I don't think they have anything that will stick." He pauses for a few moments before continuing. "But we'll see what he knows."

"And Sarah?"

"She confessed to murdering Will—or at least to helping."

"I still don't understand what Rachel's goal was with suggesting the swap…"

"No?"

"I mean, maybe she wanted to be able to frame us."

"She wanted to give the cops a reason to suspect everyone, Em."

"Yeah, I guess. And by suggesting we lie about it to the investigators… Well, it was just a matter of time before the lie caught up with us."

"That's what manipulators do. They get your buy in, in small ways. At least to start. To be blunt, she wasn't your friend."

A wave of disappointment threatens to overflow, but I bite my lip and suppress it. "What are you thinking?" Jack asks, his features etched with concern.

"Nothing," I reply, unable to look him in the eye this time around.

We sit there for a long time listening to the sound of the monitors, not speaking. I can feel Jack's eyes burning through me, and he finally says, "Em, we can fix this."

"Can we?"

His eyes meeting mine with unwavering resolve. "What choice do we have?"

A part of me wants to believe him, but the doubts still persist.

"Trust me, Em," he says, squeezing my hand with determination. "I'll do everything in my power to make it work. We both will."

"I know you have your doubts, Em. I'd be lying if I said I don't. But trust me when I say this: everything I've done, all the lives I've taken, they were necessary. It was the only way to bring some semblance of justice to a world that seems hell-bent on tearing itself apart. And as far as you and I go, I fucking refuse to be just another statistic. When something's broken, you fix it. That's always been the motive behind everything I do."

As his words sink in, I can't deny the logic behind his actions. The world is a cruel and unforgiving place, filled with people who seek only to exploit and destroy. And, while I may not fully understand or condone Jack's methods, I can see the twisted rationale that drives him.

"But you have to realize things can't go on like they are?"

"Yeah."

A flicker of relief crosses his face as he releases my hand, the warmth lingering even as our skin parts. We sit in silence, the unspoken understanding between us hanging heavily in the air.

51

Emily

I wake to the rhythmic beeping of the machines beside me. The air feels heavy with the weight of decisions yet unmade.

"Emily," Jack begins, his voice tentative as he shifts in the uncomfortable chair at my bedside. "Good. You're awake."

I study him, noting the creased lines of worry around his eyes, the way his fingers drum nervously against his thigh.

Taking a deep breath, he leans forward, the words spilling out in a hurried rush. "I've been sitting here thinking... I know having a family is important to you, and... well, I want that too, Emily. Despite the surgery, there are still ways for us to have a child together."

My heart skips a beat, hope and skepticism warring within me. "How?"

"You know me. I don't do anything without thinking three steps ahead."

"What are you saying?"

"I'm saying I have enough sperm banked that we could have thousands of kids—millions…"

My heart hammers in my chest as I consider the implications of his words. "Just one or two would do."

"Whatever you want."

"Why would you do it in the first place?"

He shrugs. "I didn't want to bring children into this messed-up world. But I also thought I might change my mind. I don't know, Em. It just seemed like a good thing to do at the time."

"Jack," I say, finally giving voice to the fear that has haunted me since my captivity. "I want to believe you. I really do. But how do I know this isn't just another one of your manipulations?"

He reaches for my hand, his touch warm and comforting. "I understand why you're skeptical, Em. All I can do is promise you that I'm serious about this. That I want to make things right between us."

His eyes hold mine. He pauses, and I feel the unspoken words lingering in the air—and I know he's thinking about my infidelity with Will.

"Even knowing I slept with Will?"

Jack's jaw tightens, but his gaze never wavers from mine. "Yeah, even that," he admits, the anger evident in his voice. "I don't want one event to be the end of us. We've had a decade of happiness, Em. It seems a little absurd to let someone like *Will* destroy it all."

"Will didn't act alone."

"Believe me, I'm aware."

"Then why did you agree to go into business with him? It's not like I hadn't warned you that it was a bad idea…and you were always so cagey about it."

"I don't like to be wrong."

"So just like that, you're willing to forgive me?"

"I know the alternative, and I don't care for it."

His determination is palpable, and a mixture of relief and

astonishment washes over me. I study his face, looking for any trace of deceit or manipulation, but all I find is sincerity. This is a side of Jack I've never seen before, and it both terrifies and comforts me.

"You aren't that forgiving, Jack," I say. "Don't forget, I know you."

He shrugs. "I don't know…maybe you've suffered enough."

"Maybe?"

"The only thing worse would be if you were dead."

"Right."

"Sometimes," he says, "you have to let people learn from their mistakes, Em."

"And what? You're saying I've learned?"

"I'm saying we both have."

"There's a part of me that doesn't believe you."

"That's why we said vows, remember?"

I nod, recalling the unwavering conviction in his voice as he'd spoken those words on our wedding day. In that moment, I had believed in us, in our ability to weather any storm that came our way. But now I'm not so sure.

"Sometimes promises are easier said than kept," I say, the weight of my own doubts pressing down on me.

"Truer words have never been spoken."

I close my eyes and drift back to sleep until eventually a nurse comes in and starts prodding at me. She checks my vital signs, smiles at Jack, flirts a little, the same as they all do.

"I need to be honest with you," Jack says when she leaves, his fingers tapping nervously on the edge of the hospital bed.

I glance at him, taking in the creases around his eyes, etched deeper than I remember. "About what?"

"About everything," he admits, chewing on his lower lip.

"All right," I reply, my heart pounding against my ribcage, unsure of what fresh revelations await me.

"First off, I'm sorry." He rubs at the back of his neck, and it's both comical and not how hard this is for him. "I'm sorry for all the times I wasn't there for you or didn't listen. I let my own desires and obsession with justice cloud my judgment."

"Jack, I—" I say, but he stops me with a raised hand. I have to admit, his groveling is not sexy, and sometimes it's best to stick with what you know.

"Please, let me finish." His eyes implore me to stay silent, so I do. "I've realized that my actions have consequences, not just for me, but for you, too. That night with Will... I pushed you into it. I wanted him dead, Em. And I intended to make it happen. I wanted you to see that I had a reason."

He hesitates, then adds, "But it was selfish. And I know we can't go on living that way. Chickens, they eventually come home to roost."

"So, what, then?"

"I think it's time to give up the life I used to lead. Try something new..."

"I liked that life," I say. "Most of it."

52

Jack

As I step into the sterile hospital room, its icy atmosphere envelops me like a shroud. I shouldn't be here, it's three in the morning, but I couldn't wait another minute to get this off my chest. Emily looks up, her eyes carrying the weight of countless sleepless nights.

"Jack," she says, her voice strained with a hint of surprise, "What are you doing here?"

My fingers fidgeting with the hem of my shirt. "I have news—I have an idea."

"All right," she answers cautiously, her green eyes flickering with curiosity and apprehension.

I pull up a chair beside her bed and sit down, every muscle in my body tense with determination. "I've been thinking a lot lately —about us, our marriage, and how we can make it better."

My words hang heavy in the air, laden with expectation.

"Okay?" Her brow furrows. "What is it?"

I lean forward, my hands clasped tightly together so I won't fidget. Emily hates any sign of weakness, but she also likes to think she has a choice. It's a tightrope walk, to be sure. "I've found a new business venture that I think has real potential. It would mean moving, but I believe it could be the fresh start we both need."

"You want to move?" Emily says, her surprise obvious. "What kind of business venture are we talking about?"

"It's an investment opportunity in a startup," I explain, my voice laced with excitement. "It's high-risk, but I've done my research, and I think it could be successful. More importantly, though, it'll give us a chance to start over."

Emily's expression shifts from shock to uncertainty as she processes the implications of my proposal.

"You could find a new job there, Em. Or not. Whatever you want. And you can make new friends, meet new people—"

"Jack, that's...a lot to take in," she admits, her fingers twisting the edge of her hospital blanket. "And it's the middle of the night."

"Look, I know it's a gamble. But I believe that if we're honest with each other and committed to making this work, I think it'll be worth it."

"All right, Jack," she says finally, her cautious optimism shining through the uncertainty. "I'm willing to give it a try—but on one condition."

"Name it."

"I want us to go to couples' therapy," Emily says firmly, her eyes meeting mine. "Before we make any big decisions, I think we need to work on our communication and figure out what we both want."

I nod slowly, feeling a sense of dread wash over me. "That's a fair condition."

Over the next few weeks, we attend therapy sessions together, unraveling the knots in our relationship and learning how to communicate better. Well, I mean, that's what we're supposed to be doing. But it's not easy—there are tears and arguments and moments where we both wonder if it's worth it. Especially when I have to confess to Emily that I killed her favorite chef.

"He made the best coq au vin!"

"Maybe," I say. "But he threatened to go to the police about the swap if I didn't give him his job back."

She's pissed for a solid day. Then she says, "Well, at least you were honest." And slowly, we start to see progress. We start to understand each other in ways we never have before.

It all starts when our man-hating therapist fires us. After I refuse to do the mind-numbing homework she assigns, she tells Em there is no hope. She has the gall to tell my wife I am not really committed. And to think I'm paying this woman to hate me and cause more problems.

Sadly, she could not be more mistaken. I have absolutely done my homework. And I hate her too.

"You're firing us?" Em echoes.

"I'm sorry," the woman says. "There's nothing more I can do."

I smile because I know my wife, and I know there's nothing she despises more than someone telling her something is impossible.

"Oh, I think there is," I say.

I take Emily's hand, and together we stand up. We look the therapist in the eye and then at each other, and, with a single nod of agreement, we make our decision.

We decide to murder her.

It starts with a plan—one that I know will work if we stick to it. As I explain my strategy, Emily's eyes fill with excitement and anticipation that I haven't seen in months. She trusts me to lead us through this, and right now, that faith gives me strength.

We start by casing the office building where our ex-therapist works, looking for any weaknesses in security. We spend days planning every detail, from what we'll wear to how we'll get away after the deed is done. Emily helps me craft an alibi so solid that even the most suspicious investigator won't be able to crack it open.

The night before our plan is set into motion, we fuck like animals and afterward we lay side by side in bed discussing what lies ahead of us. We are both scared but also exhilarated—this could be the new beginning we needed.

The next day when we arrive at the office building, everything feels surreal, like a dream that could end at any moment if someone discovers us lurking around. But no one notices as I slip inside while Emily waits outside as a lookout. My heart pounds in my ears as I make my way up the stairs toward our unsuspecting target's office door.

I push it open and there she is, slumped in her chair, a bullet wound in her head. I can't make any sense of it.

When I get back in the car and tell Emily, I'm expecting her to be just as surprised as I am, but she only shrugs and says, "I guess she had it coming."

"We're going to need a new therapist," I say.

"We've already been fired from one, Jack. And I hear that's quite a feat."

"I am not a quitter, Em."

"Fine," she says. "I'll ask around."

And then, one day, as we're walking through our new city, hand in hand, Emily turns to me and smiles. "I think we made the right choice," she says.

I look at her, more in love than ever. "I think so, too." And for the first time in a long time, I feel hopeful about our future.

53

Emily

One year later

The news of Sarah's conviction slithers into the party like a serpent, its venomous fangs sinking into my chest. I clutch my water as if it might anchor me to reality, even as the room threatens to spin out of control. Jack catches the change in my expression and saunters over, a drink in hand.

"Is everything all right, Em?" he asks, concern etched onto his handsome features.

"Justice," I breathe, swallowing hard against the lump in my throat. "I guess it has been served."

"Ah," Jack says, understanding dawning in his eyes. "Well, we were expecting a verdict any day."

"Rachel is dead," I say, unable to keep the tremor from my

voice. "And Sarah's in prison. Ava won't speak to me. Lucas, either… I don't know. Sometimes I just miss the way things used to be."

"Ava pretends to be as shocked as everyone else," Jack says. "But I'm not so sure. It's probably better you don't talk to her."

"Yeah…" I stare at the floor. "But I feel for Lucas."

"There's too much history there, Em. He lost a lot, and I'm guessing he doesn't want to be reminded of it."

"I guess not, but that doesn't make it any less sad."

Jack rubs my back. "It's the hormones."

"Speaking of, Ian will live with Sarah's parents. He'll be twenty-five by the time she's eligible for parole…"

"Every dog has its day," Jack muses, his gaze distant. "I warned you once before, didn't I?"

"Something about lying down with dogs and waking up with fleas?"

"Exactly," he says, sipping his drink. Our laughter and banter continue, a delicate dance around the truth of our past sins. One thing is clear, Jack is done with the conversation.

"Speaking of dogs," he says, lowering his voice so that only I can hear him. "You remember that man I told you about, the one who owned that dog-fighting ring?"

"I guess."

"Well, I took care of him."

My blood runs cold, and I grip my glass tighter. "You never told me."

"Consider it a surprise."

"Perhaps we should find a new therapist," I suggest, feigning hurt. "One who can help with our…unique situation."

"Or we could just keep doing what we're doing," he says playfully, and I know he means every word.

"Yeah." I rub my stomach for emphasis. "What else have we got to do?"

"Emily, darling," gushes a woman with perfectly coiffed hair and impeccably applied lipstick. "I hope I'm not interrupting anything..." She looks at Jack like he's the last glass of water in the desert. "But I must tell you, your home is simply amazing!"

"Thank you, Lorraine," I say, basking in the glow of her admiration and Jack's annoyance. It's been hard to find friends here, not that I'd ever consider Lorraine as such. "We've been so fortunate to find such a wonderful place."

"They featured it in *Architectural Digest*," Jack says before excusing himself. "I'm sure Em would love to tell you all about it."

"Indeed," she sighs wistfully, clearly envious. "And your husband, Jack—he's quite the catch."

"Isn't he just?" A wicked smile curves across my lips as my eyes drift toward him. He's across the room, mingling with our new friends, each of them captivated by his charm. Little do they know the monster hidden beneath his all-American facade.

My heart races with barely contained excitement as I set my twisted game into motion. A test of Jack's loyalty, his unwavering devotion in the face of temptation. But, also, I just really like revenge. I watch from my vantage point, the perfect blend of pleasure and unease churning in my gut.

"Jack," I call out, feigning innocence. "Lorraine was just saying how much she adores our home. Why don't you give her the grand tour?"

"Of course," he says through gritted teeth. Jack senses the game I am playing, but I know he won't be rude.

"Lead the way, Jack," Lorraine purrs, her painted nails grazing his forearm suggestively. He shoots me a look that's equal parts amusement and challenge before guiding her through the crowd.

As they disappear from view, my stomach tightens with unease. *Trust is a currency more valuable than gold.* I have messed up, will he?

"You should get off your feet," a voice interrupts my thoughts. A tall man with a crooked smile motions toward the sofa.

"Thank you." I accept the offering, forcing a smile. "I think you're quite right."

His eyebrow quirks up, sensing the tension that coils within me. "Everything all right?"

"Of course," I lie through gritted teeth, my gaze darting toward the hallway where Jack and Lorraine vanished. "Just hosting jitters."

"Ah," he nods knowingly. "Well, I must say, you're doing a fantastic job. Everyone's having a great time."

"Thank you," I manage, easing myself down. "That's very kind of you."

"You're what? Seven, eight months?"

"Seven and a half," I say, glancing at my stomach. "How'd you know?"

"My wife and I have four children."

"I can't imagine."

"No?" he says. "Well, I think you'd be surprised. We have a lot more in common than you think."

I scan the room, looking for an out.

"Anyway," he says, standing. "They're grown now. And I'm more committed to my wife than I've ever been."

"Good to know."

"We've been fired from a few marital counselors ourselves. I suppose that helps. Keeps things spicy, that's for sure."

"Do I know you?"

He smiles, and it lights up his eyes. "I'm a friend of Jack's."

"Funny," I say. "I didn't know Jack had many friends."

He sits down beside me once again, and we sit in silence for several moments before he speaks again. "He's a good egg, Emily."

"Is he?"

"Yes," he says. "But I think you know that."

"Never hurts to test things from time to time…"

"No, it doesn't," he says, standing. "How else would you know?"

When I look up again, he is gone.

As the party rages on around me, I can't help but feel like a marionette, my strings pulled taut by forces beyond my control. It's a dance as old as time, this delicate balance between love and fear, trust and betrayal. And as I watch my husband and Lorraine return, laughter spilling from their lips, I realize just how precarious my footing has become.

"If you pull that shit again," Jack says when he leans down to press a kiss to my head, "You're the one who's getting killed." He looks at me, anger seeping through his pores. "I hate that woman."

I smile. "That was the point."

Read the next Britney King thriller: *The Sickness* is https://books2read.com/thesickness Enjoy the first chapter free at the end of this book.
YOUR EXCLUSIVE FREE BOOKS ARE WAITING...
Visit britneyking.com to receive your free starter library. Easy peasy.

A NOTE FROM BRITNEY

Dear Reader,

I hope you enjoyed reading *Blood, Sweat, and Desire*.

Writing a book is an interesting adventure, it's a bit like inviting people into your brain to rummage around. *Look where my imagination took me. These are the kind of stories I like...*

That feeling is often intense and unforgettable. And mostly, a ton of fun.

With that in mind—thank you again for reading my work. I don't have the backing or the advertising dollars of big publishing, but hopefully I have something better...readers who like the same kind of stories I do. If you are one of them, please share with your friends and consider helping out by doing one (or all) of these quick things:

1. Visit my review page and write a 30 second review (even short ones make a big difference).

(http://britneyking.com/aint-too-proud-to-beg-for-reviews/)

Many readers don't realize what a difference reviews make but they make ALL the difference.

2. Drop me an email and let me know you left a review. This way I can enter you into my monthly drawing for signed paperback copies.

(hello@britneyking.com)

3. Point your psychological thriller loving friends to their free copies of my work. My favorite friends are those who introduce me to books I might like. **(http://www.britneyking.com)**

4. If you'd like to make sure you don't miss anything, to receive an email whenever I release a new title, sign up for my new release newsletter.

(https://britneyking.com/new-release-alerts/)

Thanks for helping, and for reading my work. It means a lot.

Britney King

Austin, Texas

July 2023

ABOUT THE AUTHOR

Britney King lives in Austin, Texas with her husband, children, two very literary dogs, one ridiculous cat, and a partridge in a peach tree.

When she's not wrangling the things mentioned above, she writes psychological, domestic and romantic thrillers set in suburbia.

Without a doubt, she thinks connecting with readers is the best part of this gig. You can find Britney online here:

Email: hello@britneyking.com
Web: https://britneyking.com
Facebook: https://www.facebook.com/BritneyKingAuthor
TikTok: https://www.tiktok.com/@britneyking_
Instagram: https://www.instagram.com/britneyking_/
BookBub: https://www.bookbub.com/authors/britney-king
Goodreads: https://bit.ly/BritneyKingGoodreads
Newsletter: https://britneyking.com/newsletter/

Want to make sure you never miss a release? Sign up for Britney's newsletter: https://britneyking.com/newsletter/

Happy reading.

ACKNOWLEDGMENTS

Many thanks to my family and friends for your support in my creative endeavors.

To the beta team, ARC team, and the bloggers, thank you for making this gig so much fun.

Last, but not least, thank you for reading my work. Thanks for making this dream of mine come true.

I appreciate you.

ALSO BY BRITNEY KING

**For a complete and up-to-date reading list please visit britneyking.com

Standalone Novels

Blood, Sweat, and Desire

The Sickness

Ringman

Good and Gone

Mail Order Bride

Fever Dream

The Secretary

Passerby

Kill Me Tomorrow

Savage Row

The Book Doctor

Kill, Sleep, Repeat

Room 553

HER

Around The Bend

Series

The New Hope Series

The Social Affair / Book One
The Replacement Wife / Book Two
Speak of the Devil / Book Three
The New Hope Series Box Set

The Water Series

Water Under The Bridge / Book One
Dead In The Water / Book Two
Come Hell or High Water / Book Three
The Water Series Box Set

The Bedrock Series

Bedrock / Book One
Breaking Bedrock / Book Two
Beyond Bedrock / Book Three
The Bedrock Series Box Set

The With You Series

Somewhere With You / Book One
Anywhere With You / Book Two
The With You Series Box Set

**For a complete and up-to-date reading list please visit britneyking.com

GET EXCLUSIVE MATERIAL

Looking for a bit of dark humor, chilling deception and enough suspense to keep you glued to the page? If so, visit britneyking.com to receive your free starter library. Easy peasy.

SNEAK PEEK: THE SICKNESS

Best-selling author Britney King returns with an adrenaline-fueled thriller about an unlikely array of characters and their heart-pounding plunge into the dizzying depths of madness.

March 2020: Stranded on a remote cruise ship as the pandemic ravages the world, 753 desperate passengers find themselves in a perilous situation. With no hope of docking in sight and dwindling supplies, each must fight their inner demons to survive. Among them are an eclectic mix of people—a father desperately searching for a way to save his daughter's future, an artist running from a broken past, and a hacker looking to make one last score. But what they didn't count on is the mysterious cult convention taking place on board.

With enough resources at stake to change or end lives, suspicion and fear quickly build. When bodies begin to drop, they question —is it the virus? Or is it one of them?

Don't miss this spine-tingling psychological thriller that takes readers on a white-knuckle ride to uncover the truth and find out who—*if any*—will make it off the ship alive.

COPYRIGHT

THE SICKNESS is a work of fiction. Names, characters, places, images, and incidents are products of the author's imagination or are used fictitiously and are not to be construed as real.

Any resemblance to actual events, locales, organizations, persons, living or dead, is entirely coincidental and not intended by the author. The scanning, uploading, and distribution of this book without permission is a theft of the author's intellectual property. No part of this publication may be used, shared or reproduced in any manner whatsoever without written permission except in the case of brief quotations embodied in critical articles and reviews. If you would like permission to use material from the book (other than for review purposes), please contact http://britneyking.com/contact/

Thank you for your support of the author's rights.

Hot Banana Press
Cover Design by Britney King LLC
Cover Image by Robert Thiem
Copy Editing by Librum Artis
Proofread by Proofreading by the Page

Copyright © 2023 by Britney King LLC. All Rights Reserved.

First Edition: 2023
ISBN 13: 9798215020630
ISBN 10: 8215020630

britneyking.com

THE SICKNESS

BRITNEY KING

"The road to hell is paved with good intentions."

— Proverb

PROLOGUE

The world is spinning too fast for me to make any sense of it. Fear and desperation choke the air as a steady buzz of panicked whispers fill the background like static. The wind whips my hair across my face as I stand on the deck, the ocean crashing beneath me. A thousand eyes seem to be upon me.

My fellow passengers are in chaos, their faces wild and terror-stricken as they grab supplies and flee from the horror. The ship isn't as full as it once was, but it's still crowded, and people race in all directions, panic spreading like wildfire. Everywhere I look, people are in a state of desperation. Some run, some cower, and some simply stand frozen, as if waiting for the inevitable.

I search for Dad, and I feel my own panic rise within me. I see hundreds of faces, but none are his.

Then I hear him calling out my name.

"Abby!"

"Dad?"

"Abby!"

Finally, I spot him across the deck, arms full of water bottles, and I exhale the breath I'd been holding. He motions for me to move forward as planned, and I dash toward the bread line, thirst scratching at my throat after a full day without water. Over my shoulder, I watch my dad weave through the crowd. He has that same look on his face he had when he told me about this trip—determination mixed with dread—and I know what's going through his head: We should have never gotten on this ship.

Roger Atkins has never been a cruise ship kind of guy, but considering the circumstance, what could he say?

"It'll be an adventure, I guess," he'd finally said, and he was right.

"Next!" a woman shouts, and I move forward in line.

I hand over my ration card to a lady with dead eyes. Children aren't supposed to be on deck when rations are dispersed, but I'm not most children. I'm sixteen, though I might as well be eighty. People frequently utter words like "last resort" and "little hope" when they think I'm not listening. One look at me and it goes without saying.

I grab two loaves of bread and can't help the satisfied grin that washes over my face. We have water and we have bread. Everything is right in the world again. I glance toward my dad in triumph, but something else captures my eye.

An eerie stillness has draped the deck like a blanket, and an icy chill runs down my spine.

A man is wielding a gun. He's pointing it straight at the crowd. My heart stops, and my breath catches in my throat.

I scan the deck, but Dad is not where I last saw him. I don't see him anywhere. Fear courses through me like icy nails, freezing me in place. I know I should run, but where? A single gunshot slices through the air—I scream in sheer terror.

I am not the only one.

Everything happens so fast. I don't have time to run. I don't even have time to think. One shot evolves into many. Bullets whip through the air in all directions. The man turns and aims at me and instinctively, I hit the deck. My vision blurs, but not before I see drops of my blood splatter around me. Liquid heat blankets my skin and searing pain rips through my stomach. Then everything goes dark.

When I stir back to consciousness, the air is ringing with sirens and frantic screams. Burning pain radiates through my chest with every breath, and my pulse races, a reminder I'm still alive.

One thought thunders in my head: *find Dad.*

I push onto my elbows and survey the carnage around me. Bodies are strewn across the deck like broken dolls, some silent and still, others writhing in pain as fellow passengers scavenge their rations. The wood beneath them is drenched in blood, a river of red that covers the world in crimson.

I close my eyes for a moment and will the darkness to take me. I don't want to die like this, but I don't want to live this way either.

Someone tugs at the loaves of bread that I have gripped firmly, and my eyes snap open. A wild-eyed woman pries at my fingers, but I refuse to let go. "I have children."

"I am a child," I bellow, clutching the bread to my chest. The woman turns and walks away without a word. Just once she looks back, for what I don't know—I assume to see if I'm dead yet.

I give her the finger. That's when I see him wading through the sea of people, shouting my name. He doesn't stop until he's reached me. Relief is evident in his eyes, but they widen when he sees the scarlet stains on my shirt.

Dad pulls me into his arms and whispers words of comfort. For a moment, all I feel is relief—relief that we are both alive.

He looks into my eyes and smiles softly, "Abby, it'll be all right."

"My stomach—"

He reaches down and peels the blood-soaked shirt away from my skin. "It's not that bad," he says, after exhaling a heavy breath. "You're gonna be fine."

I nod. And stupidly, I believe him.

BRITNEY KING

READ MORE:
https://books2read.com/thesickness

Printed in Great Britain
by Amazon